A Tangled Web

*To Amandalemaster —
What would I do
without you? I treasure
our friendship, "Foo-Foo"!*

A Tangled Web

*Thank you so much for
your support and always
promoting me — Big Hugs!*

Ingrid

Ingrid McLaughlin Taylor

*Ingrid McLaughlin Taylor
October 6, 2006*

Dedication

**To Chuck Taylor
for the happiest five years of my life**

Acknowledgements

A multitude of thanks to my mother, Christa McLaughlin, for support, encouragement and being my #1 fan. A heartfelt thank you to gentle readers Carol Cleveland, Angela Filbeck, Tina Vyborny, Phyllis Lundvall, Tiffany Fredericksen, Christy Dannaldson; and the Divine Miss C (Constance Whiston) for her daily dose of cheer and inspiration, over the wall.

There are so many wonderful friends at Bass Pro Corporate to thank for their support and efforts to promote my work: Ann Creller and Suella Gonzales are the most amazing and generous hostesses; my special ladies in the Import/Export Compliance department; Shirley Drake, Amanda LeMaster, Melanie Childers and Jan Allmeyer, also known as Cinco La Femme. They are a daily source of inspiration and joy.

A special note of thanks to author and friend, Janet Elaine Smith, for sharing her tools of the trade, promotional expertise and passion for the craft. No one tells a story quite like Janet.

Prologue

At first she couldn't escape the pain. It wound throughout her body and crept into her soul. Crying didn't help; it just made the sensation more intense. The salt from her tears stung the raw areas on her face. During brief moments of lucid thought she tried hard to focus her mind and remember who she was. After an eternity, a vision in muted green appeared to her—a blurry smiley face that came to comfort and soothe, but first she paid the price of another sting. A second later the pain left her body, as if the smiley face had pulled the plug and drained it all away.

She opened her eyes, blinking into the dark, trying to focus on a television set that was suspended from the ceiling in a corner of the room. She looked around, her thoughts not quite making contact with reality. There was a man leaning onto her bed from a chair that had been pulled close to the railing. He was asleep in this awkward position, his head on his arm, her hand wrapped in his.

The door to her room pushed open and a man entered, dressed in green hospital scrubs. He carried a metal tray and set it on the blanket beside her. Without raising his head, he started a familiar chatter.

"How're we doin' this evenin', Miss April? Guess what it's doin' today? Snowing! That's right, just when we thought spring was..."

"Fine, thanks." April managed a hoarse croak. "Water. Please."

The metal tray clattered to the floor, vials and syringes scattering. When she focused in his direction, his eyes were wide as they looked directly into hers and his face broke into a familiar smile.

1

"Now you just sit tight, Miss April. I'll be right back with your doctor." Smiley face bent to pick up the spilled items, scurried out of her room, and sped down the hall.

Chapter 1

"Have you *lost* your mind?" Patti's outburst echoed through the small bookstore. April set her sandwich down, her eyes scanning the room to see if anyone had overheard her. "Come on, Pat, I've known him for months. We talk over the Internet every night. You've even talked to him yourself." She defended herself in hushed tones, even though there didn't appear to be any customers in the store.

"I thought you were crazy when you started talking to this guy, and you know it! If he's so great, then why is he home alone every night?" Patti obviously didn't care if a customer walked in, judging from the volume of her verbal assault. "Why hasn't he got a girlfriend? How do you know he's not married?"

"We've talked at different times of the day and no one but him has ever answered the phone or been in the background. He lives alone, just like he said. He's a decent guy. He goes to church all the time. I believe what he says, Patti, and frankly, I really don't care what you think." April stood up. "If I don't meet him, I could be passing up the best thing that ever happened to me. I'm sorry you can't understand that." April tossed the remainder of her lunch into a brown paper bag and mashed it furiously between her hands. She had lost her appetite and was fighting back angry tears. Criticism from her only friend ran deep. *Why can't Patti understand that God has finally given me someone of my own to love?* She hadn't told Patti how intense her feelings were, afraid of this very thing happening, but she hoped Patti would be happy for her and encourage the relationship, or at the very least understand it. April dropped the crumpled lunch bag into a trash can as she hurried through the fiction section of the bookstore to the ladies' room.

"April...Oh, *come on*, April!" Patti stood and watched April hurry away. *The poor kid is clueless when it comes to men.* Only April wasn't a kid anymore. She was almost thirty years old and still possessed an awkward shyness that most ten-year-old girls had long outgrown. Patti sat down and picked at her potato chips, remembering the April who had come to her shop five years ago. The woman who applied for the part-time job was dressed like a little grade school girl. She wore a plaid pleated skirt, white shirt, navy sweater, matching navy knee socks, and brown leather loafers. Of medium height and slight build, she had worn her shoulder-length brown hair parted in the middle and fastened with barrettes. Her large brown eyes matched the color of her hair, but she infrequently made eye contact. Not darting, deceitful eyes, but rather the kind that had no confidence. She seemed beaten down, like an abandoned puppy you wanted to scoop up into your arms and protect. In the five years April had worked with her, Patti had seen a miraculous transformation as April turned into an attractive, competent woman. Theirs was one of those talk-showed-to-death "co-dependent" relationships. Childless, Patti found someone to mother, and "April the Mouse" found someone to help her break free from her debilitating shyness.

April bolted the bathroom door and ran the cold water. Looking into the mirror, she checked to see if her eyelids had swollen, relieved that they hadn't. She splashed cold water on her eyes anyway. She still had to make it until closing time. Patti had given the other two employees Christmas Eve off, since April was always willing to work. Her life was the bookstore and the small world that Patti had opened up for her. Patti and her husband Max included April in their lives as if she were their daughter. There was no other family for April. She was the only adopted child of an older couple. She couldn't remember her adopted dad at all, and her adopted mother had been sick after their first couple of years together. April's physical needs had been taken care of, but never any emotional ones. *April the Mouse.* The cold water took the sting from her eyes, as well as Patti's remarks. *Why doesn't Patti understand that at long last God has given me someone of my own to love?*

April had two hours left to try and convince Patti that she was doing the right thing. She was going to meet her future husband face-to-face.

Her heart raced at the thought.

Chapter Two

April heard the telephone ring as she sprinted up the stairs to her apartment. She fumbled with the key until the lock clicked open and the door swung wide. She dropped her things on the kitchen table and ran to pick up the phone. Nothing but a dial tone. Her heart sank. She knew it had been Kenny on the other end of the line, but she also knew he'd call again in a few minutes. They'd developed a kind of ESP. She could even tell when he was thinking about her. She retraced her steps into the kitchen, straightening out the items she had dumped in a heap onto the kitchen table. She pushed the door closed and locked it.

Kenny would call back any minute, so if she hurried she'd have a cup of coffee ready to sip during their talk. While she had few modern gadgets, April's absolute favorite was her Bunn coffeemaker that took all of three minutes to make a pot. Her one indulgence was flavored coffees, and she made a special blend of her own—mixing regular, hazelnut and vanilla and topping it off with lots of cream. It was like having dessert every day. The rich, sweet aroma of her special treat soon filled the tiny apartment. April took her favorite mug out of the cabinet and filled it with the steaming brown liquid, placing it next to the telephone by the couch. She changed into a warm pair of sweats and her favorite fuzzy slippers. From her nightstand she picked up the romance novel she read from each night before she went to bed. Hugging it to her chest, she walked to the couch and sat down. She pulled her legs beneath her as she snuggled up for the night, ready to spend Christmas Eve with a good book, a good cup of coffee, and the deep, soothing voice of Kenny Colt, her gift from God.

April woke with a jolt. It was 11:45 p.m. and the party next door was breaking up. Revelers were shouting drunken "good-byes" in the hallway. She picked up the book that had dropped to the floor when she fell asleep and replaced the bookmark where she last remembered reading. Her heart was heavy as she realized Kenny hadn't called her on Christmas Eve. He'd made sure she would be home that evening just so he could call her. *He promised.* For the first time in five years, April had not spent the Christmas holiday with Patti and Max, and all for nothing. Kenny hadn't called and she'd hurt her only friends. She felt hot tears rolling down her cheeks and had a terrifying thought. *What if he's been in an accident?* Maybe something awful had happened and he couldn't get to a phone. After all, he was *so* dependable. He *always* called when he said he would. Yes, something must have happened! She raced to the kitchen and dumped the contents of her purse on the kitchen table, finding her tiny address book. She thumbed the pages quickly to the "C" section and hurried back to the couch, berating herself for not memorizing his number. She started to dial, suddenly very nervous about making this call. *What if there was another woman in his life? What if Patti was right and he'd been lying to her all along?* The tears kept on rolling and she wiped them away with her sleeve. She *had* to know. She began dialing his number again. The phone answered on the fifth ring.

An older woman was laughing when she answered, "Merry Christmas! Santa's helper speaking." More laughter. April started to replace the receiver, but slowly raised the phone back to her ear.

"May I speak to Kenny, please?" April asked quietly. She heard the sounds of a party in the background. A stereo was playing too loudly to the accompaniment of laughter and raised voices.

"Hello? Santa Claus here." Kenny was laughing, too.

"It's April." Her heart stopped when she heard his voice. He hadn't been in an accident. His phone worked fine. He was having a party after making her miss Christmas Eve with Patti and Max. April felt like a fool, and her tears began in earnest "Hey, baby. How's my girl?" Kenny said. "Sure do miss you, honey."

"You said you'd call. I—I thought maybe you'd been in an accident or something and couldn't get to a phone." She felt hollow inside, putting mental pictures to the background sounds she heard. She wanted to scream, but the hurt was too deep. She'd been forgotten; she was just someone to pass a lonely night with on the Internet. She'd betrayed her friends for an illusion. What an idiot she was!

"Baby, I *couldn't* call. Half the church is here. They brought a tree and potluck supper. I couldn't take away their joy at doing a good deed by telling them I couldn't let them in because I had a *call* to make, now could I? What kind of Christian would take away someone's joy like that?" Kenny was interrupted several times and April began to feel guilty for her negative thoughts.

"Baby, I was sure you'd understand when I called in the morning. Do you want to talk to my pastor? He's standin' here right now. There's nothing bad goin' on here, I swear. Baby?" April sat still, not knowing what to say. She didn't understand how he could ruin her night and expect her to understand. On the other hand, she knew he was a good Christian. After all, his pastor was there. "Oh, Kenny...I don't know what to say. I'm sorry for thinking the worst. I feel so bad for letting Patti and Max down this year. I know I hurt them, and then I thought you'd forgotten about me. It's hard being alone on Christmas Eve."

"You're never alone, baby. I'm always there with you, even

if it's only in spirit. And in a few days it'll be in person. I told you God spoke to me, April. I know you're the woman He's sent me to be my wife. Don't ever think bad thoughts about me, baby--or about us. Patti and Max are Satan's way of ruining things for us. You just put those two out of your mind. By New Year's we'll be planning our wedding, baby. You're gonna have a new life with a whole new family—a church family—the way things are supposed to be." Kenny had taken on his "sermon voice," like he did whenever he got steamed up about things. April smiled at the images his words conjured up in her head. Her heart felt all warm and fuzzy again.

"You're right, Kenny. I'm sorry for ruining your party. That's so sweet of your church to be there with you for Christmas. Satan always ruins things by putting bad thoughts in my head. Don't worry, I'm fine. Missing you is all that's wrong with me."

"That's my girl." Kenny's deep voice took away all her fears and bad feelings. She'd been unfair to him, judging him like that.

"You know I love you, baby, and I'm waiting right here for you, honey." April closed her eyes and smiled.

"I love you, too, Kenny. Merry Christmas," she whispered. She fell asleep with a smile on her face, images of her sweetheart in her dreams.

Chapter Three

April carefully packed the last of her few belongings into the Ford Escort. In a way, she was glad she didn't have many possessions; it made the winter move that much easier. Lugging the heavy boxes, she worked up quite a sweat going up and down the two flights of stairs that led to her apartment. All that was left was for her to have a final cup of coffee, pack the coffeemaker into its box and call Kenny to let him know she was on her way. Little shivers of fear periodically jostled their way through her body. Those "what ifs" that Satan invariably put in her head would surface, and she had to force them from her mind. Kenny reminded her, over and over, that God had spoken to his heart, and more than anything, she wanted a man of God— someone she could trust with her heart. Someone who would be true. The sound of a "yoo-hoo" and a knock on the apartment door jolted her from her daydreams. April got up and opened the door to gaze into Patti's tear-streaked face. Patti dropped the packages she held in her hands, and the two women embraced.

"Oh, kiddo, you have no idea how much I'm going to miss you," sobbed Patti, squeezing April even tighter in a bear hug. "Max sends his love, too." Patti pulled away and searched April's eyes. "April, we can't part in anger. We've been friends way too long. I can't help but worry about what you're doing. I have nothing against Kenny, except that he's taking you away from us. And until I meet him face-to-face, I'll worry that he could be some sort of psycho. You've heard the horror stories on the news." Patti took a tissue out of her pocket and wiped her eyes. "But I'm not here to try and change your mind or talk you out of going. I know you've made up your mind. I need to know that we'll always be friends and that you'll stay in touch with me. This Christmas has been so lonely without you,

April."

"I've missed you so much, too. Please don't be upset. Be happy for me. Kenny's a great guy. You'll see. He's so sweet and kind. He really, truly cares about me." April led Patti into the kitchen. She poured coffee into two Styrofoam cups and sat down across from her dearest friend. "Patti, he's asked me to marry him. Marry him! He's not trying to get me there for sex. He wants a *real* relationship. He's very religious and says our relationship will be a triangle, with God at the head. He means what he says, Patti. I can feel it in my heart." April wrapped her hands around the cup and smiled into Patti's eyes. Patti placed her hands around April's, not wanting to break the connection, hoping that some common sense would rub off.

"I'm going to miss your wonderful coffee, too." She smiled as she looked into April's eyes. "I'll miss you more than you can imagine. You're my best worker, best friend and best coffee maker. I can't imagine you not being in the shop when I re-open on January 2nd. I guess a new year will really be a new beginning for both of us, won't it?" Patti leaned across the table and held the younger woman's gaze. "April, there's one thing I want you to promise me. Promise me you'll keep in touch. Let me know that you're safe and happy. If you do that, I swear I won't worry or try to talk you into coming back. But I need to know you're okay."

"Oh, Patti. Please understand. I *have* to do this. I have to be with him. It's like my heart is full and I have joy in my life. I've prayed and prayed about it and feel I have God's blessing. I want to have your blessing, too. And yes, I'll keep in touch. Once you and Kenny meet, he'll be so happy to have you and Max as friends. You'll see. He's a loner like I am. I'm sure we'll be down to visit you, and you'll visit us, too. You'll always be welcome wherever I live. You know that, don't you?" April smiled at Patti and pulled a card from her purse.

She handed it to Patti. "See? Great minds think alike. I was going to stop on my way out of town and give you my phone number and address in Oakwood. Kenny says he's the only 'Colt' in the phone book, so it shouldn't be too hard to find us. I'd never forget about you, Patti, or lose our friendship over a silly argument. This is something that I just *have* to do." The rest of the conversation was of old times and traveling routes and how long April thought her trip would take. They talked until the last drop of coffee was drained and then unplugged April's treasured coffeemaker and rinsed out the pot before packing it carefully in the remaining box. They hugged, amidst heartfelt good wishes. April walked Patti to her car and watched her through tears that blurred her vision as she drove away. She had packed every single possession into the Escort. For the last time, she walked slowly up the two flights of stairs and fondly remembered the cozy little nest this sparsely furnished apartment had been. She took another look around each room to make certain she hadn't forgotten any items. She then dialed Kenny's number and happily told him Patti had "seen the light" and she had made peace with her best friend. She was, at long last, ready to start her new life.

Chapter Four

The wind blew steady and cold on the little car, but April was snug and warm inside, driving slowly and carefully southwest toward Oakwood. Joy and fear took turns with her emotions, as daydreams of life with Kenny meandered through her mind. She reminisced of the first time they met on the Internet, how their relationship had grown from "buddies" to wanting to share each other's lives. She smiled to herself, recalling different times Patti had told her that someday there would be a man in her life. "God has made a mate for each person on the earth," she said. The trick was in finding him. By the time April was twenty she didn't hold out much hope of marrying. She felt herself too plain, and certainly much too boring. Her childhood had been spent in relative isolation and she wasn't very comfortable with people. Books became her passion. Men from real life never were as brave or honest or caring as the men in the novels she loved to read. After dinner most evenings she would curl up on her couch and read until she fell asleep. Books were so much better than real life. Books didn't judge or criticize. Rich or poor, beautiful or not, books could take you anywhere in the world. And so she willingly traveled the globe, learned some foreign languages on audio-books, solved mysteries and conquered men's hearts—all from the comfort of her couch.

She lived alone, but never felt lonely until she came to expect messages from her Internet friend. One rainy evening she joined a mystery chat room and made a new friend. She was intrigued by the insight of the new member called "Ponylover." She thought it was a woman at first, but when he explained that he used "pony" instead of his real last name of "Colt," and that he was "a lover, not a fighter," she thought he was rather clever. Soon they left the chat room and began to exchange email addresses. Two weeks after racing home night after night to see if he'd sent her an email, he told her he wanted to hear her voice. April didn't hesitate to give Kenny her unlisted number. They immediately went off-line and April sat by the telephone, a sudden fear growing in the pit of her stomach as she wondered if he would like the sound of her voice. When the phone rang, she answered as brightly as she could and was amazed at the confidence she felt as he not only approved of her voice, but told her such nice things about her ability to understand the written word. He liked the fact that she was a loner and said he was a loner, too. He asked if it would be okay if he called her once a week or so. Her heart leapt in her chest and April, at long last, could say that she knew what it felt like to fall in love.

April began buying little cards and gifts she thought Kenny might enjoy and appreciate. She baked him cookies and searched endlessly for new books she thought he would like. Mailing a weekly "goodie" package that she hoped would endear her to his heart became an almost obsessive ritual. But it was all worth it, because for the first time in her life she felt like she was walking on clouds, with Kenny in her thoughts and in her heart. He told her that he was a religious man and would end his phone calls by saying a prayer before they hung up. April would add "amen" when he was finished, to be sure he knew she agreed with all that he had prayed for. She went to sleep each night knowing that a man of God would never lie or cheat or be unkind. She found the perfect man and she would do her very best to be the perfect woman for him. It hadn't taken much longer after Kenny began ending their calls with prayer that he first told April how God had spoken to him. "God has touched my heart," he said, and April would be his wife. Kenny then asked April to marry him. Once again, without hesitation, April said "Yes."

April thought of the details of their whirlwind courtship at least a million times during her lone drive. She passed a sign that read "Welcome to Oakwood, Missouri" and a thrill of adrenaline washed over her. She was in her new hometown. All of a sudden the trip hadn't taken long enough, and fear eased its way into her mind. The "what-ifs" were almost crippling. She remembered Kenny's warning that Satan would try and split them up before they could ever be together. She pulled over to the side of the main road and lowered her forehead until it rested on the steering wheel. She prayed with all her heart that God had orchestrated their relationship, because she was here with all her earthly possessions and there was no turning back.

April navigated around the winding roads, using the handwritten map Kenny had sent to her last week. He said he wanted their first meeting to be at his country church, because if they had God's blessing from their first moment together there would be no doubt of a happy union. After their initial meeting she would follow him home rather than try to find her way alone along the unpaved backwoods roads to his house, nestled even deeper in the woods.

Chapter Five

To April's horror, the parking lot of the little country church was filled with cars. As she found a space and pulled in, a young boy came around the rear of the building and ran to her car. He stood at her window and smiled. April unrolled the window, letting in the frosty air.

"Are you Miss April?" the child asked. He shivered as he stood by her door. Dressed only in slacks and a sweater, he wrapped thin arms around himself, his breath making smoky puffs in the freezing temperatures.

"Yes, I'm April. Did Kenny send you to meet me?" she asked, trying not to show her disappointment to the child. As he shook his head up and down, April told him to come around to the passenger side of the car. She took her purse and a few other items she kept within easy reach on the passenger seat and put them in the back, then reached over to unlock the door. "Sit in here with me for a minute while I get my things together."

The little fellow did as he was told and ran around the back side of the car. He got quickly in, his apple-red cheeks and partly toothless grin making April smile. "Thank you, Miss April. It's awful cold outside."

"What's your name and where's your coat?" she asked as she wondered who would let their child out, improperly dressed, in this weather.

"I'm Jacob," he said proudly. "I left my coat inside 'cause I wanted to be the first one to meet you, Miss April. Uncle Kenny told me that you're gonna be my aunt and that's why you're getting married." Jacob wiped his nose on his sleeve and added, "I think you're pretty." He smiled at her again and April managed to smile back. She was sadly disappointed and scared. Kenny told her it would only be the two of them when they first met. There were at least twenty cars in the parking lot. If

19

whole families had come to meet her there could be an army of people jammed into the little church, all wanting to scrutinize her. April's heart was hammering. She had spent her entire life avoiding people. She wasn't sure she could get out of the car— or even if she wanted to. Kenny *knew* she was a loner, that she was shy. How could he do this?

"Are you okay, Miss April? Uncle Kenny said you might feel funny with everybody here."

"I get nervous around crowds, Jacob. I wanted to meet your Uncle Kenny quietly before I met everyone else. I guess I'm kind of scared."

"Don't worry, Miss April. I like most everybody here. And the food's good."

"What do you mean, the food's good?" April pulled her gaze from the church building to her companion.

"Everybody brought food. We're having a welcoming dinner. It's 'specially for you." He smiled his toothless grin at her.

April laughed and ruffled his hair. "Well, if you'll walk me in, I guess I'll be okay."

"I can sit next to you if you want," Jacob offered.

"That'd be great. Thanks." April said a silent prayer and gathered her winter coat from the back seat. She tilted the rearview mirror and smoothed her hair. "I guess I'm as ready as I'll ever be."

As Jacob got out, she prayed again for strength. Determined to go through with meeting Kenny's friends, she focused her mind on the little boy. "Oh, Jacob, you're shivering. Here, we'll share my coat." She pulled on her long down jacket and hugged Jacob to her side as she locked the car and slipped the keys into her purse. Together, they quickly ran to the rear of the building, trying to stay warm in the icy late afternoon air.

Entering the building from the back door, April removed her coat and found an empty hook to hang it on. The warmth of the church and wonderful smell of home-cooked food permeated the building.

"I'll tell Uncle Kenny you're here, Miss April." Jacob beamed at her one last time, bounded up the stairs of the cloak room and disappeared behind a heavy curtain.

Bellowing at the top of his lungs, April heard Jacob proudly proclaim, "Miss April's here!" All chatter stopped. The only sound she could hear was the pounding of her own heart. It was the moment of truth. She could run out the door she just entered, get in her car and drive away, returning to her safe haven and boring life—or, she could endure the next few hours and see if they had the wonderful future she and Kenny had envisioned in all the emails, letters and talks they had shared over the past few months. She took a deep breath and slowly climbed the steps, determined to meet her new world face-to-face.

Chapter Six

April steeled herself to face the unknown and parted the heavy curtain that divided the cloak room from the main area of the little church. She stepped into a thick, uncomfortable silence and for a long moment; her heart stopped. There were *so many* faces staring at her—some smiling, others not. She stood rooted to the top step. An eternity passed as she scanned the crowd, searching for the face that had stared out at her from her computer screen every day for the last several months. Breaking through the sea of unfamiliar faces, little Jacob ran up to her and grabbed her trembling hand. "See? I told you she was pretty!" He smiled. There was light laughter and people resumed talking among themselves as Jacob led April into the midst of the room. A tall, pencil-thin woman with stern features and steel-gray hair piled high atop her head was the first to make an introduction.

"I'm Pastor Wilson's wife, Marian." April was offered a limp handshake and a smile that didn't make it all the way to the older woman's eyes. She was grateful for the courtesy of a greeting, but was painfully aware that Kenny wasn't in the crowd. She couldn't put her feelings into words, but it seemed as if everyone in the room was as uneasy as she was.

"Thank you, Marian. I'm April. Is-isn't Kenny here? " April stammered, self-consciously looking around the room once more. The woman's dull, blue-eyed stare intimidated April, as she cringed under the unwelcome scrutiny of a stranger.

"The elders are talking with him now. We understand that you don't share our faith." Marian's piercing stare was boring a hole through what little bravado April had mustered before walking up the stairs.

"I don't exactly know what your faith is, but I do know Kenny loves this church and he's a Christian. I'm a Christian, too. I-I wasn't raised in a church-going home, but Kenny and I have talked it all out and we'll be coming here regularly," April offered. Maybe that was the reluctance she felt in the air. She wasn't one of "them" yet.

"I'll be instructing you in your role as a Christian wife. I hope you're a fast learner, because I've only got a week to teach you." Marian crossed her arms over her chest, holding onto her elbows, the classic "no nonsense" pose. Marian's eyes darted to a spot behind April's head.

"I'll try. To do my best, I mean." April glanced around the room again, wondering what the pastor's wife was talking about. How different could the House of God's rules be from other churches? She turned to see what Marian was looking at, and there *he* was, in the midst of a half a dozen men walking towards her. The Kenny of her dreams! Their eyes locked and Kenny held out his arms to her, gathering her in a quick embrace.

"How's my girl?" he whispered in her ear. He put his arm around her shoulders, giving her a squeeze every now and then as he introduced April to the men of the church. April smiled politely and shook hands with the House of God's elders. She was almost afraid to look at him as she stood self-consciously by his side. He was shorter than she'd expected. He told her he was 5'10", but she was certain he was barely inches taller than her own 5'6". A million little things were bombarding her senses as she took in the glasses he wore and the obvious dentures that didn't fit his mouth properly. Her heart was pounding and nothing seemed real as she tucked her wild thoughts away to a distant corner of her mind and tried desperately to focus on being a polite newcomer to the group.

April looked up to see Pastor Wilson make a barely perceptible signal to Marian, who nodded to her husband and then quieted the church group. Another nod from Pastor Wilson and Marian stood primly at his side as he made a quick announcement. "We'll all have plenty of time for visiting with Kenny's bride-to-be during dinner. Is everyone hungry?" With the group murmuring agreement, Pastor and Marian Wilson led the group downstairs to the basement, where an elaborate meal awaited. At the head of long, rectangular tables that had been placed together end-to-end, two chairs sat under an extravagantly decorated arch, with pink and blue crepe paper ribbons and bows adorning the seats of honor. Jacob pointed to a hand-lettered sign that proclaimed "Congratulations, Kenny and April." The two were seated at the head of the table and the rest of the group took their places, the pastor and Marian sitting across from Kenny and April at the far end of the long table.

Not used to being the center of attention, April was relieved when the group finally settled down and began dishing out food, their attention focused on the meal instead of her. She desperately wished that Kenny had come to meet her alone so they could have talked. She had waited months to be near him, to be his wife. But he hadn't met her like they planned, and even worse, he left her to fend for herself with a room full of strangers, knowing how painfully shy she was. He hadn't even kissed her yet. In her daydreams of their first meeting, she'd imagined they would be lost in a passionate embrace and locked in a kiss that would end only when they had to come up for air. This was nothing like her fantasy. She snapped out of her reverie as she felt the weight of Kenny's head leaning on her shoulder. "Are you happy, baby?" he whispered. She turned and gave him a weak smile as the pastor stood to give the blessing over the food. Pastor Wilson thanked the good Lord for this joyous occasion to gather His chosen together to enjoy the fellowship and food of His bounty, as Kenny reached for April's hand under the table and gave it a squeeze. His simple act of acceptance erased any doubts and uneasy feelings that started to fester, and she immediately warmed with the realization that in time she would be a part of this little church family.

When the pastor sat down and picked up his fork, the rest of the little congregation followed suit, and soon there was the comforting din of flatware clinking on stoneware plates amid the happy noise of laughing children. The chatter was interrupted when the pastor rose and tapped his fork against his water glass.

"I think everyone will want to join me in welcoming April to the House of God, where we look forward to having her join us as a sister in the work of the Lord." Applause and cheers erupted as all eyes turned to the favored couple. "We also want to congratulate Kenny and April on their upcoming union in the Lord, which I believe...er...is this coming Saturday. Is that right, Marian?" Marian nodded to her husband and then gave a prim nod in April's direction. "Marian will lead the elders' wives in giving April instruction as to her Christian duties as a wife and as a member of the congregation. We'll all meet here next Saturday at noon and all present will be privileged to watch the grace of God conferred on Kenny and April as they are joined in the holiest of God's plans for mankind: the union of man and wife." The pastor was orating now, obviously pleased with the sound of his own voice. April kept a smile plastered on her face, nodding politely when catching someone's eye, making pleasant comments about the food the ladies had prepared, all the while wanting the evening to end. She hadn't been able to get a good look at Kenny as she played the part of a reluctant actress, feeling as if she were on stage while trying her best to make a good first impression. The only thing keeping her going through the long evening was the certainty that it would end and she and Kenny would be alone to talk and get to know each other. She still battled the butterflies in her stomach when the dinner, at long last, ground to a welcome close. As the ladies and children gathered up dirty dishes and took them into the kitchen area, Marian refused April's offer of help.

"No, April, this is your night with Kenny. You two visit while we get ready to go. I'll let you know when Pastor Wilson and I are ready to leave." Marian's mood seemed a bit brighter as she took a dish filled with serving spoons from April and headed toward the kitchen. Kenny was at the door, waving goodbye to Jacob's family as April shyly approached him.

"Hi, baby. Did you have a good time?" Kenny asked as he took both of her hands in his.

"I guess I'm getting over my shock. I didn't think I'd be able to handle myself in front of a room full of strangers, Kenny. I wasn't expecting this at all." April's soft-spoken words and downcast eyes belied the way she felt inside. Kenny had betrayed her trust. "I thought we were going to spend our first couple of days alone, getting to know each. Alone."

Kenny lifted her chin and looked into her eyes. "Now, baby, I couldn't help what happened tonight. Marian told Pastor of our plans and she insisted on this engagement supper. How could I tell her 'no' and take away her joy?"

April looked into Kenny's eyes and saw the handsome face she only knew from her computer screen until a couple of hours ago. Her heart was beating wildly once again. He really was handsome. She'd get used to his height and glasses and teeth. After all, those were superficial things. He was so kind to Pastor and Marian. He was a good Christian man, and she was lucky to have found him, so very lucky he wanted her for his wife.

"I'm sorry. I'm so nervous around crowds."

"Well, baby, this is your new family. You're gonna have to get used to them. We'll be seeing them twice on Sunday, and every Wednesday night, too. You'll fit right in. Don't you worry about a thing, darlin'." He took her in his arms and lightly brushed her lips with his own. "I'm so glad you're here, baby. I've been missing you so much."

"Oh, Kenny, I've missed you, too." April's heart was so full of love for this man that God had chosen for her. He took her hand and led her back to the cloak room. For a moment they were alone and Kenny took the opportunity to give April the first real kiss she had ever experienced. Her breath came in short gasps as her body responded to his. When he finally released her from his embrace, she was stunned by the effect he had on her senses. "I love you so much," she whispered in his ear. He squeezed her hand and winked at her as Pastor Wilson and Marian joined them in the cloak room.

"How are our lovebirds doing? Did you both enjoy the party?" the pastor asked.

"Oh, yes. Thank you so much." April gushed. "It was so thoughtful of you both."

"Well, April, we hope you'll enjoy being a part of our family. Our church is a tight-knit, loving group and we want what's best for you and Kenny." The pastor smiled as he helped his wife with her coat. "We'll be waiting for you in the car. Kenny, be sure you lock up." And with that, Pastor Wilson and Marian stepped out into the chilly night.

"Now, baby, there's something else I have to tell you…" Kenny took April by her shoulders, ignoring the confused look on her face, and gazed deep into her eyes. "I know this isn't what we had planned, but it's for the best." While April's thoughts reminded her that nothing in this meeting had gone according to plan, her heart was still beating from the kiss that had crushed her lips a moment ago, and despite her reawakened doubts and disappointment, she nodded like an obedient little girl.

Chapter Seven

"Idle hands are the work of the devil! You'd best be getting out of bed, Miss April." A stern Marian shook April, scaring her out of her wits. "I've already let you sleep late enough." April bolted upright, not knowing where she was—only certain that she wasn't in her apartment. Then reality set in. The Wilson's had refused to let Kenny and April set a bad example for the congregation by allowing the unmarried couple to sleep under the same roof, un-chaperoned, before their wedding day. April felt hurt and disappointed when Kenny broke the news to her last night, but she obediently followed the Wilsons home and dragged her suitcase into their spare bedroom. Worn out from her day of driving in winter weather, she fell into a troubled sleep as soon as her head hit the pillow, and she hadn't had time to think things through. She tossed and turned into the wee hours, when blissfully, around 3:00 a.m. she finally sank into the peaceful release of sleep.

April mumbled a "Good morning" to Marian and followed the older woman down the hall, bringing clothes and toiletries to the bathroom. "You won't be needing all that smelly stuff. And there'll be no makeup either. We don't believe in our women looking like floozies painted up for men, causing them to have filthy thoughts over. At the House of God we look and behave like God's own Christians."

"Thank you." April was now fully awake and felt as though she had made the biggest mistake of her life by coming to Oakwood. Among the unfamiliarity of a strange house and strange people, Marian's angry voice grated on her already-fragile nerves.   Closing the bathroom door, she set her things on a little table next to the commode, trying her best not to give way to tears at how her dreams of a new life and happy marriage had turned out. She decided that after she'd gotten showered and dressed she would ask Marian for directions to Kenny's house and then stop to tell him goodbye on her way back home. Maybe Patti and Max would forgive her and let her stay with them until she could find another apartment. April felt her face coloring at the thought of going back to Patti and Max like a puppy with its tail between its legs, especially when she remembered how hateful she had acted when Patti tried to talk some sense into her.

April towel-dried her hair and stepped out of the shower, wrapping the small cloth around her. She brushed out the tangles and picked up the blow dryer. Plugging the cord into an outlet near the sink, she bent over, fluffing her hair with her free hand, as she held the dryer in the other. She was suddenly aware of a pair of men's shoes standing in the bathroom in front of her. She jerked up, nearly losing the towel in her fright. "Oh, my God! What do you want? Get out! Please!" April dropped the blow dryer in an attempt to keep herself covered. She looked frantically into Pastor Wilson's eyes—hungry eyes that had traveled the length of her legs and back up to her face. She took small steps backward until her calves hit the side of the tub. The pastor reached down and picked up the still-running blow dryer. He flicked the switch to silence it and laid it back on the bathroom vanity.

"You should be ashamed of your evil thoughts, young woman!" the pastor roared, his bushy white eyebrows furrowed in an uneven row. "You didn't answer when Marian called. Since there's nothing wrong, hurry on up. We waited breakfast for you, and I'm hungry." He turned on his heel and slammed the bathroom door behind him. April could hear the muffled voices of the pastor and Marian as she felt the breath she was holding come out in a huge whoosh. Now she had *really* done it! How could she have thought the pastor had had bad intentions? She was so ashamed of herself, distrusting these

people that had let a stranger into their home. She must be a
terribly ungrateful person, finding fault with Kenny and being
unappreciative toward the pastor and his wife. April dried off
and finished dressing. She took her personal items from the
bathroom and made her way back to the bedroom and neatly
repacked her belongings into her suitcase. In deference to the
Wilsons' wishes she wore no makeup, only a dab of lip gloss to
keep her lips from chapping in the cold weather. Satisfied that
her appearance wouldn't offend anyone, she quickly made the
bed and walked sheepishly into the kitchen.

"So you think Pastor'd be interested in the likes of you, eh?"
Marian gave April the once over as she snorted in disgust at
their temporary houseguest.

"I'm so sorry, Pastor Wilson. You startled me. I didn't mean
to offend either of you." April stood still behind a kitchen chair
and hung her head.

"Come over here, young lady. " Pastor Wilson took April's
hand in a fatherly fashion when she came near. "This will be a
new life for you. It's probably very different from what you're
used to, but there's one thing I can assure you of—you can trust
any one of the elders in our congregation with your life. Not
one of the ordained men, most especially me, would ever lay a
hand on you or any other female that's not one of our wives. Is
that clear?" April nodded her head, still unable to look the
pastor in the eye, her face enflamed in embarrassment. "We're
very serious about God around here. That's why we kept you
and Kenny apart last night. There will be no fornicating while
you're a member of the House of God. Now, let me give the
blessing so we can enjoy Marian's cooking. Go sit down."
April walked back to the chair she had stood behind and sat
down. She looked up at the pastor, with tears in her eyes, and
managed a smile as he began the blessing for breakfast. She
then glanced over at Marian, but the older woman's head was

bent, hands folded primly on her lap. After the pastor muttered "Amen," Marian passed the hotcakes to her husband, then to April, and finally herself.

"I hope you'll...that is, I..." April stammered.

"We'll not speak of it any more, April," Marian snapped, swallowing her scowl along with her breakfast. "Eat your breakfast. We've got a lot of work to do—you and I—before Kenny comes to take you to lunch."

Despite her earlier certainty that she was going back home, April's heart leapt at the news that Kenny was coming for her soon. Now maybe they could have a serious heart-to-heart talk and everything would be all right. April dug into her breakfast with a renewed appetite, as she daydreamed once again of her fairy-tale love.

Chapter Eight

April put the last of the dried breakfast dishes into the cupboard as Marian had instructed her. She gently closed the door to the highly polished oak cabinet while Marian removed the crisp, white linen apron from her waist, folded it neatly and draped it over one of the chair backs. April stood and watched the clipped, precise movements the older woman made as she bustled about the kitchen. The house was so clean, it was almost uncomfortable. Every piece of living room furniture was covered with fitted plastic protection and April was afraid to touch anything for fear of leaving fingerprints or footprints. Even Marian, for that matter, seemed uncomfortable in her home. April felt increasingly awkward and shy the moment the pastor left the house to "tend his flock." Marian was neither a warm nor a gracious woman, but it was clear nothing would come between her and her "Christian duty."

"Get your Bible so we can study before you go traipsing off!" Marian barked at April.

"Uh-I, I don't have a Bible," April said, once again looking down at her hands.

"What do you mean, you don't have a Bible? You mean you didn't bring it with you?" Marian audibly gasped, clutching at the neckline of her dress as she looked in disbelief at April.

"No, I mean I've never had a Bible." April cringed at the expression coming from across the table. "I figured Kenny would teach me what I need to know and I'd read from his."

"I've never heard of anyone not having a Bible! I don't suppose you've ever been to church either?" Marian, in total disbelief, was giving April the most unnerving stare.

"I've been a couple of times with friends," April offered, not knowing what to expect from Marian. Clearly the woman was in shock at the thought of having a heathen in her home.

"Well, that explains how you came to meet Kenny through the Internet. The devil's own playground! Does Kenny know this?" Marian was beside herself with indignation, still not quite sure it wasn't all some strange joke.

"Yes, he knows. He said we'll be spending a lot of time at the church." April focused on the back of Marian's elaborate hairdo as it left the kitchen and disappeared around the far corner of the living room. She looked up at the clock, but it was only 8:30 a.m. Kenny wouldn't be coming for her until lunchtime. She walked to the kitchen door and pressed her face against the cool glass, taking in the winter scene in front of her. The Wilson's driveway was flanked by two long rectangles, one on either side of the garage entrance, now covered with fluffy snow. She imagined the yard brilliant with flowers during the spring and summer months and then thought better of her fantasy of the Wilson's yard; flowers were probably too cheerful for Marian Wilson! April sighed, wishing for this week to come to a rapid end.

"Don't stand there all day. We've got work to do!" Marian's high-pitched voice broke through April's reverie. She turned and saw Marian holding two thick, black books in front of her. One was well-worn and obviously used quite often. The other was still wrapped in plastic. "Go on, open it up. Let's get started, although I hardly know where to begin!"

As April pulled the plastic wrapping from the new Bible, she smiled at Marian, hoping to break through the wall of unpleasantness between them. Marian shook her head at the young woman across the table. April thumbed through the gilt-edged, spider-web-thin pages in her hand. What a joy to hold a new book!

"It's yours now. Put your name in it so you don't lose it."

"Oh, Marian, thank you!" April gushed. She smiled again and took the pen Marian offered and neatly wrote "April Stover" on the inside cover. "I should probably wait until Saturday to add 'Colt' on the end, shouldn't I? " April lifted her eyebrows for Marian's answer and saw the dull blue eyes welling with tears. She had no idea what the tears meant, but reached over and patted Marian's hand. It was quickly withdrawn from the table as Marian leafed through the pages of her own dog-eared volume.

"Well, since you don't know the Bible, I guess we'll start with the Ten Commandments and go on to the Beatitudes, although I'd wanted to start with Proverbs 31. I'd better ask Pastor what to do. I've never met anyone in a church that didn't know their Bible! This is not the way things are usually done."

Somehow, the two women made it through the next couple of hours, April soaking up Marian's instructions like a sponge. The adrenaline rush from being constantly on edge apparently made her a good student and Marian seemed pleased with April's success in memorizing some of the different verses. When they heard a vehicle pull into the driveway, April instantly sat straighter and smiled again at Marian.

"Thank you for being my teacher, Marian. I had no idea the Bible could be so interesting."

"Well, it'll be even more interesting tomorrow. We'll stop for now and let you get on your way with Kenny." Marian closed her Bible with a snap, stood away from the table and waved to Kenny, who stood with his nose pressed to the glass, making an idiotic face before entering.

"Hey, baby. How's my girl?" Kenny came through the door with a big grin and spread his arms out to April. She stood slowly and embraced him, burying her head in the collar of his jacket. He bent to kiss her and once again her lips tingled with the anticipation of what his kiss promised.

"I'm fine, honey. I've been studying with Marian. Look. She gave me my own new Bible." April showed it to Kenny, beaming under his approval. "I'm sure she'll have her hands full with me for a student." They laughed and kissed again, longer this time, until a tapping foot and a loud "a-hem!" broke them apart.

"Now, Marian, you know you're my best girl!" Kenny went to Marian, putting his arm around her and kissed her on the cheek.

"Oh, cut that out!" Marian giggled like a school girl at Kenny's flirtation as she hurried them out of the house. "I expect you to stay for dinner tonight, Kenny, so make sure you have April back by six o'clock."

"Baby, do you mind if we take your car?" Kenny asked, nuzzling April's ear as they walked with arms around each other toward the garage.

"No. Of course not." She dug in her coat pocket for her keys and Kenny took them from her hand.

"I like to do the driving. You don't mind, do you, baby?" Kenny asked, flashing his smile at her.

April was a little annoyed at the ease with which he helped himself to her car, but she didn't say anything. She was probably more uptight than she realized, so she returned his smile as he held the passenger door open for her. Once inside, she leaned over and unlocked the driver's door. He climbed in and gave her another quick kiss, then adjusted the seat and mirrors while the Escort was warming up. "Nice little car you've got here. 'Our' car I should say. In a few days, 'what's mine is yours and what's yours is mine.' I'm so happy you're here, baby."

April took the opportunity to finally get a good look at Kenny. He was a good-looking man, appearing healthy and fit. She could still feel his last embrace imprinted on her body. He wasn't as tall as he claimed, but he was a comfortable fit for her, the right height when they hugged, so what did a couple of inches matter? He had beautiful, kind eyes. So what was it about him that left her feeling uncertain? She couldn't put her finger on the little niggling doubt, so she tucked it away in a dark corner of her mind and tried to concentrate on getting to know him. Alone at last, they could talk.

"Where do you want to eat, baby? I'm not a rich man, but we can go somewhere besides McDonald's." Kenny reached for her hand as they came to a stoplight in the center of the little town.

"I don't really care, Kenny. You decide. And McDonald's is fine. I'm not picky."

"I have to eat at the same time everyday or I get shaky, April. I can't waste too much time deciding where to go!" He seemed annoyed with her, even though his words came out through smiling lips.

"I don't know where else to suggest, Kenny. I haven't been to Oakwood before." April stated the obvious and hoped they weren't going to have their first argument. He pulled into the parking lot of a fried chicken place and removed the keys from the ignition. As April put her hand on the door to let herself out, he shouted "no" and ran around to her side of the car to open the door. "Why, thank you, Kenny! I don't believe I've ever had a man open a car door for me before."

"Get used to it, darlin', 'cus I'm going to treat you like a queen." He pocketed her keys and took her hand as they walked into the little restaurant. It was a cheery place, with red and white checkered tablecloths and hanging plants in the window of each table. They found a booth in a quiet corner and Kenny helped her remove her coat. April was torn between feeling extra special and feeling smothered with his fawning over her. She supposed he was doing his best to make a good impression, or maybe she simply wasn't used to being treated like a lady. As she slid into the booth he said, "Keep going, darlin', I want to sit next to you." April obediently slid over, but felt self-conscious at his smothering nearness.

"I can't get a good look at you if you're next to me," she said, smiling sweetly at him, hoping he'd move to the other side of the booth.

"You'll have plenty of time for lookin' at me after we're married. I want you by my side, April. And I want the world to know that you're my wife. Equal—side by side. That's the way it's going to be." The waitress came by and brought silverware and water. Kenny ordered for both of them and handed the menus back to the waitress.

"I'm glad we have a chance to talk, Kenny. I want to make sure I'm the person you were expecting to meet. Are you disappointed at all?"

"Disappointed?" He shouted the word and April immediately felt her ears burning, along with the rest of her face. "No, I'm not disappointed. Why would you even think that? You're a beautiful woman, April. I'll be proud to have you as my wife."

"Thank you, Kenny." April kept her head down to avoid the eyes that were looking in their direction. She made a mental note to watch what she said to him, because he seemed oblivious to his surroundings. "And I'll be proud to be Mrs. Colt."

The waitress came with salads and set them down. In that moment, she decided that Kenny was speaking from his heart, and although too loudly for her comfort, she wouldn't let his "rough edges" color her judgment. When he bowed his head to bless their food, she was certain he was the man God wanted her to spend her life with. Yes, he would just take a little getting used to. She squeezed his hand as he said "Amen" and enjoyed a pleasant lunch.

Chapter Nine

The next two days passed much the same as the first. April listened to Marian's instructions from the pages of their Bibles, learning how to be a good Christian wife for Kenny. Her awkwardness around Marian and the pastor hadn't eased very much as she witnessed the older couple's interpretation of the Christian woman's role of submission to her husband. April silently thanked the Author of her Bible for giving her sweet Kenny, instead of the pastor, who, although he praised Marian's abilities to others, rarely had a kind word for his wife. No matter now hard Marian tried to please the pastor by keeping an immaculate home, doing the secretarial duties for the church, cooking wonderful meals and catering to his every need and whim, April never heard a kind word or saw a loving gesture for Marian. To add to Marian's daily burden she now had the responsibility of teaching April about religion from the ground up. Each evening after the dinner dishes had been washed and put away Marian would retire to the living room for a few moments to spend by herself, while Pastor would sit across from April and ask questions from the day's lessons. He seemed satisfied that Marian was an adequate teacher from April's responses.

"You're doing very well, young lady," the pastor said as he closed his Bible. "What evening did Kenny set aside for you to be baptized? We don't have much time left until Saturday."

"Baptized? Kenny didn't mention anything about that." April sighed. "He has meetings every night this week, I think." April fidgeted in her chair, uncomfortable with talking about Kenny. He had told her time and again that he was a private person and didn't want her discussing him with any of their friends or family. He told her one of the reasons he was attracted to her was that she had no family to interfere with their relationship. They only needed to trust each other, and no one else.

The pastor looked at April and slowly shook his head. "Kenny hasn't had a serious discussion with you yet, has he? Do you know what the meetings are for?"

"No, he never said, and I didn't ask. I assumed they were work related."

"Do you know what he does for a living?"

"He has a repair shop in town. We haven't had time for me to see it yet, but I will— soon." April realized that she hadn't seen anything other than Kenny himself. She must seem like an absolute fool to the pastor and Marian, leaving behind everything and everyone she held dear to marry a man she didn't know a thing about. "Pastor, I trust Kenny. We'll get to all the loose ends before Saturday."

"I hardly think of your baptism as a 'loose end,' April." The pastor was obviously disturbed as he rose from the table. "Baptism, as with marriage, is not something you enter into willy-nilly. They are both serious undertakings that will affect the rest of your life. I suggest you do some serious soul-searching and praying this evening before you commit to something you regret." The pastor stomped off, muttering under his breath. April was stunned at his reaction. Kenny spoke so highly of Pastor Wilson, but it was apparent that the pastor didn't think very highly of Kenny. No, that wasn't it at all! It was Kenny's choice of a wife that had soured the pastor's mood, April mused. That must be the reason that Marian couldn't warm up to her, either. April got up from the kitchen table and absently pushed her chair in. She walked slowly to the guest room, the need to talk with Kenny growing with each passing moment. She couldn't get in her car and go to him. He still had her car from the first time they'd had lunch. He said he wanted all her things in her new home ready and waiting when she moved in. Even if she had kept her car at the Wilson's, she had no idea where he lived. For a crippling moment, she felt totally isolated and alone. If only she could talk to Patti about what was happening. But she still wasn't ready to admit to her best friend that she might have made a foolish mistake.

Determined not to feel sorry for herself, but rather to try even harder to win the friendship of the pastor and Marian, April came to a decision. With her plan in mind, she changed into a pretty plum knit skirt and sweater set. She put pearl barrettes in her hair, scooping her dark hair away from either side of her face. In the few short days she had spent with Marian, she learned that if you dressed in the right colors it would bring out the blush in your cheeks and the color of your eyes. She smiled at her reflection in the mirror atop the beautiful old oak dresser in her room.

The sound of cars tires crunching on the snow in the driveway, followed by the opening and closing of the kitchen door, signaled Kenny's arrival. April picked up her purse and Bible and draped her coat over her arm as she walked quickly to greet her man.

A low wolf whistle greeted her entry into the kitchen. "Thank you." April blushed as she went into Kenny's open arms.

"Baby, you look beautiful, as always." Kenny's smile lit up the room and April suspected from the looks he was giving her that it had more to do with the day her clothes would come off, rather than what she was wearing. Her blush deepened when he pulled her bottom to him as they embraced and he made certain she could feel his arousal though her skirt.

"Kenny! Stop it!" she said in a frantic whisper, pushing him away and smoothing her skirt.

The pastor chose that moment to enter the kitchen and April was grateful to see Marian following behind. Kenny had never touched her in a sexual way until now, and she was shocked that he would choose this particular time and place to express his desire for her.

"Should I make a pot of coffee, Pastor?" Marian addressed her husband, but her eyes darted from Kenny to April when she asked. The pastor nodded and took his seat at the kitchen table, as Marian bustled about filling the coffee maker with coffee grounds and water, then gathered cups, saucers and napkins.

"Actually, Pastor, I'd like to take a couple of hours this evening to talk with Kenny. We haven't discussed our finances yet. I haven't seen my new home or Kenny's business. I know this is a church night and church is important, but my marriage is a lifetime decision, so I'm hoping I won't offend anyone by our missing tonight's meeting." The room was silent for a long moment as April looked Pastor straight in the eye and noticed the corner of his mouth turn upward, almost in a smile. She looked at Marian and Kenny in turn, and smiled to herself when she noticed that both of their mouths formed perfect "O's".

"I don't think that would be appropriate tonight, baby." Kenny pulled out a chair for April and then one for himself as he said to Marian, "I'd love a cup."

"Nonsense," the pastor huffed. "Tonight will be as good a night as any. April will have to be baptized by Friday for your Saturday wedding. That only leaves tonight and tomorrow for her to tie up all her loose ends, doesn't it? I think the good Lord will forgive you both if you miss one night of scripture reading."

Marian poured the pastor's coffee, then Kenny's, April's, and finally her own. She sat primly erect, holding her cup between both hands, looking over the rim at the pastor, then at April.

"Well, my goodness," she said, pausing to take a tentative sip of the fragrant, steaming liquid. "Things are moving right along, aren't they?"

Chapter Ten

"*Why* are you doing this to me?" Kenny shouted after he got in behind the wheel and both doors had closed. His eyes blazed in anger as they bored a hole through April, waiting for her answer.

"What? What did I do?" April cringed at his anger.

"You made me look like a *fool* in front of Pastor and Marian! Don't think for a *second* that I don't know what you're up to!" He shook his finger an inch from April's nose and she feared that he was going to strike her. She squirmed as far into the door as she could, tears welling up in her eyes.

"I--I don't know what you're talking about!" she cried.

"*Nobody* messes up my routine! Do you hear me? *Nobody!*" His rage was causing the veins in his head and neck to bulge. Little flecks of spittle flew from his mouth. "And don't you ever, *ever* change plans without asking me first!" He raised both fists over the steering wheel and slammed them down repeatedly. His jaw muscles were visible as he clenched his teeth in a fit so intense that April thought he might have a heart attack.

April cowered, covering her face with her hands, bracing for an attack. Her mind raced, unable to concentrate on what had happened to trigger his outburst. Every square inch of her body was shaking from his verbal assault. They sat for a few minutes in relative silence, his harsh, heavy breathing and her muffled sobs the only sounds that were magnified within the confines of the little car. April timidly peeked up when her heart finally stopped racing. The car felt muggy and damp inside; the windows were completely fogged up.

"Baby, I'm so sorry. Can you ever forgive me?" Kenny sat perfectly still in the driver's seat, staring straight ahead and whispered his apology.

She tried to speak, but no words came. Kenny reached out his hand to move the hair from her eyes and she shrank like a wounded animal from his touch. "Oh, baby, no. Please, God, don't let this ruin things between us." He slid as close to April as he could and took her awkwardly in his arms. He held her with one hand and smoothed her hair with the other, whispering "I'm sorry" over and over until he felt April relax in his embrace.

"You okay, baby? Please, baby, talk to me." Kenny was weeping now and April could tell that he was as horrified by his outburst as she was. "Baby, I love you so much. I need you. Please forgive me. I'm begging you, April." He had lowered his head as he cried and now looked up at her with so much hurt and need that April's heart broke for him. She caressed his face for a few moments until he seemed to have his emotions together, pushing himself upright behind the steering wheel once again. "Let's go home, baby. I'll tell you everything when we get there."

April turned forward in her seat. "Yes, Kenny. Let's go home," she whispered.

The black of the winter night sky disappeared as a canopy of twinkling stars emerged from behind a dark rolling cloud. April smiled to herself, realizing that God sometimes answered prayers in very dramatic ways. She had prayed for a man who needed her. Her prayers had been answered. The Escort backed out of the Wilson's driveway, stopping for a second as Kenny shifted gears and headed slowly down the narrow gravel road that led deeper into the Missouri woods. The road wound around hills and dipped into valleys as Kenny navigated the pot-holed path. Rounding a bend, April saw the green glow of many eyes, the headlights of the car reflected in their surprised stares. In an instant, all that could be seen were the fluttering white tails of a herd of deer as they bounded away into the night.

"Oh, it's so beautiful and peaceful out here, Kenny." April cooed. "I love it."

Kenny's hand reached for hers in the dark and he gave it a quick squeeze. "Exactly the way our lives will be, sweetheart. You'll see." Kenny held her hand tighter as the headlights illuminated a rough wooden fence with hand-lettered warnings written in black paint across the horizontal boards. "No Trespassing." "Keep Out." "No Hunting." The signs warned stray hunters and woodsmen alike. Kenny stopped the car. "I'll be just a minute, darlin'. I'll check the mail and get the gate."

Kenny went to the country mailbox that stood at the outside of the headlights' reach and removed a couple of envelopes. As he walked to the latch at the gate, he turned and swung it wide. April could see nothing but the odd and faintly spooky silhouettes of leafless trees ahead of her. Kenny climbed back into the car and drove ahead a scant 30 feet into what appeared to be a wide path. He got out once again and April watched him in the side view mirror, thinking how rugged and handsome he looked, how close she felt to him now, despite—or maybe because of—his vulnerability. His deep need for her aroused her maternal instincts. He closed and latched the gate and as he turned to make his way to the car, April gasped in fright, her hand flying to her mouth. In the red glow of the Escort's taillights, his features distorted in shadow, he appeared to float toward her on the black of night, as hideous as a demon.

Chapter Eleven

April continued to tremble as they came to the end of the gravel drive, the image of Kenny as a demon still vivid in her mind. The headlights illuminated a weathered log cabin with a small porch along the front. A dull orange glow emanated from the windows and the smell of acrid wood smoke permeated the crisp night air. Kenny turned off the ignition and killed the lights as clouds rolled between the car and the moonlit sky, enveloping them in an inky blackness. When he held open the car door, the only sound April heard was the beating of her heart. She felt spooked again—spooked by the total isolation, the absolute quiet of the forest. Their steps from the car to the porch were magnified as snow crunched underfoot, breaking through the soundless night.

Kenny unlocked a massive padlock and stood aside as April entered, his hand pushing gently on the small of her back. He followed close behind, closing the door and replacing the padlock on an inside hasp, snapping it locked. April's skin prickled in nervous anticipation, not knowing what to expect next. He had locked them both inside with a padlock. There was no way out for her unless he chose to let her go. Was this going to be her fantasy come true--the fantasy of a love-filled life with a wonderful man in a seemingly enchanted forest? Or was she being kept prisoner by some evil power, masquerading as a religious man in the middle of a wooden prison where no one could hear her cries for help? Kenny left her by the front door as he went to the source of the orange glow, pushed aside the fireplace screen and added a couple of logs to the fire. April stood, mesmerized by the flames licking to life as they brightened the room enough for her to make out her surroundings. The cabin was simply furnished, and as Kenny turned the lights on she was pleased with how homey and comfortable it felt.

"Well, this is our castle, darlin'. What do you think?" Kenny spread his arms, palms up, eager for April's reaction.

"It's like an old cabin from the movies or something. So old fashioned." April spun around in delight as Kenny helped her out of her coat. "Oh, Kenny, I love it!"

"I'll make us some coffee while you look around, baby. I've got your coffeemaker all plugged in and ready to go." Kenny gave April a kiss and held her tightly for a moment, relieved at her approval of the cabin. He hung their coats on fat wooden pegs that were off to the side of the heavy front door, then went to the kitchen, leaving April to explore her new surroundings. Wooden latticework divided the room where Kenny was pouring water into a coffeepot from the tap. There was a cozy little dining area. Hand-stitched samplers with Bible quotations hung on the walls and a dish was filled with a colorful array of silk flowers sat on the table. In the corner was a computer desk, with lots of shelves filled to overflowing with papers, CD's, and a printer. On the far wall were a television and several bookcases, a huge dark recliner in the corner, with a reading lamp and end table next to it. The far end of the living room boasted a huge native stone fireplace that blazed and crackled, making a cheerful sound. A comfortable couch, with several throw pillows on it, sat across from the fireplace, and to the right of the hearth was a smallish alcove, where she discovered the bathroom. She was facing a tub with the shower curtain thrown back and she could see that new plumbing had been installed. April smiled again. Kenny preferred baths, but April had told him she liked to shower. The gleaming new hardware in the tub attested to his love for her. She went from the bathroom to the fireplace and warmed her hands for a moment. A painting full of cherubs and flowers sat in an ornately gilded frame, surrounded by framed black and white photographs on the mantel. Kenny joined her by the fireplace. He enveloped her in his arms and whispered that he loved her, then led her gently by the hand behind the great stone fireplace. There was a double bed in the center of the room, with a headboard that held double reading lamps and several shelves and small drawers. On either side of the bed was a nightstand, each holding an oil lamp and a box of wooden matches. One had a change dish, assorted framed photographs and a comb.

"This'll be our favorite room, baby. You'd better plan on spendin' a lot of time in here." Hands that held her in a loving embrace moved to her shoulders and started rubbing gently, then with more force. They slid down her arms to her breasts, while he kissed the back of her neck. April's breathing came in short gasps and she whirled sharply around, swatting at his hands.

"Stop it!" She stood glaring at him, her hands trying to cover her chest. "You promised to talk to me, not rape me!"

"Oh, come on, darlin'. Don't be playin' hard to get with me." His face distorted in anger and he reached for her again. April stormed past him and ran to the front door.

"Don't you dare touch me like that, Kenny Colt! You're the one who made the big deal about religion and love and doing things properly, and now you're acting like some, some..."

"What? Like a man who has needs?" Kenny sneered. His mood had changed in an instant. "You wore that outfit so I'd want you. You wanted to be alone with me. This is your doin', baby, not mine. I'm just followin' your lead."

"That's right. I wanted to see what my home was going to look like. I wanted to know how we were going to handle our finances. Those meetings you've gone to every night—if we're going to be married, you need to start telling me what's going on. Why is it that you've taken my car from me?" Spurred on by raw nerves, April asserted herself, her fear being replaced by anger. She put her hands on her hips and stood defiantly in front of Kenny. "I want to know everything about you. Until I know exactly what I'm getting into, I will not be treated like some tramp you brought home for an evening's entertainment!"

"Looks like I got me a wildcat. I like that, baby." Kenny's menacing smirk unnerved April. One minute he was a perfect gentleman, and the next minute she was afraid to be with him. And here she was, padlocked inside. There was no way she could get out if he didn't open the lock. Panic was starting to mount, her heart beating wildly.

"Yep, you sure are a spitfire, I'll give you that, baby!" He backed off, grinning, and pulled out a chair for her at the table, laughing as he walked into the kitchen to retrieve the coffeepot and cups. "Go on an' sit down. I'll keep my distance 'til we've had our talk, but waitin' til Saturday night? Well, I don't know if I can do that."

April hesitated before making her way to the table. He was in control and he knew it. She took a seat, as Kenny placed a cup and spoon, milk and sugar, in front of her. He was still chuckling as he turned his chair around and straddled it to face her, seeming to enjoy her discomfort.

"Okay. It's you and me, baby, so ask away. I'll tell you everything you want to know and I promise to tell you the truth." He took a sip from his cup and reached for April's hand across the table. She kept her grip on the cup in front of her, unwilling to have any contact with him. As frantic as she felt, she knew she had to keep her head on straight. Somehow, she had to get him to take her back to the pastor and Marian. She had to get her car keys. Why hadn't she listened to Patti?

"Okay. Well, then, you can start by telling me about the meetings." April fidgeted with her cup. She looked at him, then away. His mood seemed to have changed again. She tried to look beyond Kenny to locate a back door, even as she felt his eyes bore a hole through her own. There was no escape in sight.

"I'm a recovering addict—drugs and alcohol. I have to go to rehab meetings. Sometimes I go once a week, sometimes every night. It depends on how stressed out I get." He tried to touch her hand again, and this time April sat rigid, but she didn't pull her hand away.

Drugs and alcohol? Was that the reason for his crazy mood swings?

"What--what kind of drugs?" April asked. She refused to make eye contact with him as her eyes searched the little cabin again for a way out.

"Look at me, babe. I know what you're doin'. There ain't no way out of here, except with me. You need to relax." Kenny clasped her hand, commanding her attention. She looked into the eyes of a stranger—a stranger that was smiling at her and for the moment, acting calm and sane, except that he wasn't about to let her go. "When I was younger I got into all kinds of stuff. But I never hurt nobody. Got hooked on drugs and liked my liquor. I started drinkin', then snortin' coke and got carried away. One of the conditions of my parole is that I stay in rehab."

"Parole?" April gasped. "Why didn't you tell me any of this before? You mean you were *in jail*?" Her heart started beating wildly again. Now he wasn't only devious and moody, he was a felon as well. Tears started to well up in April's eyes and she started feeling light-headed and dizzy. Her stomach felt like sharp knives were being pressed into it. As she broke away from Kenny's grip she stood up, knocking her chair over. Clutching at her stomach, she looked toward Kenny for help and saw him still smiling at her.

"Well, you never asked, baby. Need a little help there, darlin'?" He sneered. "Here, baby, let's go lie down for a little while." She felt his arms around her waist and shoulders as he half-dragged, half-carried her toward the bed. Her knees had turned to jelly and her tongue felt swollen within her mouth as her stomach churned and she began to dry heave.

She tried to push him away, but the room was spinning so fast she couldn't stand up straight. Her last thought was the realization that Kenny had poisoned her coffee. As the room faded into a thick, black fog, she heard pounding on the heavy wooden door. The scream that started in her mind never made it to her throat as another wave of cramps caused her to double over. With a muffled moan, she collapsed, unconscious, onto the bed.

Chapter Twelve

April fought the overwhelming drowsiness, willing her mind to awaken. She could hear voices, but could not make out the words. She slowly came to her senses, her stomach still in painful knots from whatever drug Kenny had given her. When she tried to sit up, the throbbing in her temples knocked her back down and she involuntarily let out a low moan. There was a brief silence and then the voices rose in anger. She slid her legs from the bed and forced herself upright, using every ounce of strength she possessed. Inch by inch, she finally stood, steadying herself with one hand on the wall. She shuffled as quietly as she could toward the kitchen. Was the visitor a friend or foe? All she knew was that she had to get through the door before Kenny padlocked it again. She pitched herself to the lattice divider and saw Kenny in a heated debate with Pastor Wilson.

"Pastor!" She cried out, doubling over in agony as sharp pains ripped through her stomach. "Help...me." The last of April's weak plea was lost as she fell to her knees.

"See? What'd I tell you? She's a stinking drunk, Pastor. Look at her. She was high before we even got through the front door. I was letting her sleep it off before bringing her back to your place." With his back to the pastor, Kenny walked over to April and gave her a self-satisfied grin. Bending over, he grabbed her under the arms and jerked her roughly to her feet. Her stomach heaved again. "Now ain't this just pitiful? This woman needs the Almighty's help. Don't you worry, Pastor. I'll take care of her."

"Pastor... please. Help me," April mumbled. She tried to get her feet underneath her so she could stand alone. "He's done something..." She couldn't finish her sentence as the pain wracked her body again.

Pastor Wilson stood with his hat in his hand. "I guess I'll leave you to it, Kenny. Under the circumstances, I don't think she'll be in any condition to break any of God's laws that she hasn't already broken." Putting a hand on April's shoulder, he said, "Marian and I will be praying for you, April, but I've got to tell you that I'm terribly disappointed. Your behavior is intolerable." He patted her shoulder, jarring her throbbing head with the movement.

"Don't leave me," April mumbled through her tears. "Please, Pastor." Another wave of nausea hit her and she mumbled "bathroom." Kenny carried her into the bathroom and left her kneeling by the toilet. He pulled the door closed behind him as April started heaving once again.

Kenny turned to face the pastor. "Now don't you two lose any sleep over her. If anyone knows how to handle drunks, I surely do."

The pastor nodded in agreement and put on his hat and heavy overcoat, readying to leave.

"Well, at least if you change your mind about marrying her no one will fault you. With the progress you've made in your own life, you don't need to be brought back down. Like I said, we'll be praying for you both tonight." The pastor sighed, clasping Kenny's shoulder. The two solemnly shook hands. Kenny nodded his head and stood in the doorway, watching the older man make his way to the end of the drive. When he reached the gate and was finally out of sight, Kenny switched off the outside lights, pushed the door closed and securely fastened the padlock. He leaned back against the door and let out a long gleeful howl.

"Yee-haw! Baby, that was one close call!" He laughed out loud and slapped his thigh, stopping suddenly, aware that April was still in the bathroom. He went to the door and rapped lightly with his knuckles. "Ready or not, here I come," he sang in a voice that sent chills down April's spine. April was sitting on the floor between the tub and the toilet, her legs drawn up, her head on a towel that lay across her knees.

"Baby, you're not looking so good." He bent over her and gently lifted her face in his hands. He seemed surprised at her condition, noticing that her eyes were glazed and red-rimmed. "Oh, baby, now don't be *cryin'*." He kissed the top of her forehead. "You need some rest tonight, darlin'. I'll sleep on the couch and you can stay in here or have the bed. It's up to you." He stood up. "I'll get you a tee shirt, ok?"

April felt so awful she didn't care what he did to her now. Most of the drug seemed to be out of her system, but she wasn't going to let Kenny know it. Her eyes were swollen from the tears she had cried with the realization that the pastor wasn't going to help her, or even believe that she needed any help. Pastor Wilson thought she was a drunk—or worse. April was trapped in this house with a madman. All the niggling little doubts she had overlooked when they talked over the Internet were coming back to haunt her: the incredible possessiveness, how he didn't want her having any friends or family, his insistence on getting married right away, how he told her over and over that "God told him" or "the Lord touched my heart." What a fool she'd been! She wanted so badly to believe that he was her gift from God that she hadn't listened to her own instincts--or to Patti's warnings. Hot tears spilled down her cheeks anew as the door opened.

"Here you go, baby. When you're ready you can put these on." He placed a neatly folded gray tee shirt and black sweatpants on the bathroom vanity, then placed something on top of the clothes. "Here's a new toothbrush. Whatever you'll need's in the medicine cabinet." She felt his eyes as he stared down at her for a long moment. "I'd kiss you goodnight, but you really need to wash up. You're a mess." He reached in the medicine cabinet and took out a blue toothbrush and squeezed out a dab of toothpaste. April watched as he meticulously replaced the cap on the tube and put it back in the cabinet. She had noticed earlier that he seemed unusually neat for a bachelor. Now she realized he had to have the structure and order in his life, as many recovering alcoholics and addicts need, to function. He busied himself with meticulously washing his face and combing his hair and hummed softly, seeming to forget she was in the room. Suddenly he turned and smiled down at her. "See you in the morning, baby. You need to get up by six and make my breakfast. I leave for work at seven." He turned and walked out of the bathroom, pulling the door closed behind him.

April was stunned. Her thoughts were crystal clear now. She wouldn't make a move until she was certain he was in a deep sleep. She heard noises in the bedroom and a moment later there was rustling as he shifted his weight on the couch. She couldn't leave the bathroom without being seen. Praying he was a sound sleeper, she decided to wait at least half an hour before leaving the relative safety of the bathroom to try to locate his keys. In the meantime, she would plan her escape.

April jerked awake, her head snapping back against the wall. It took a moment to orient herself to her surroundings. Tonight's ordeal had exhausted her and she fell asleep on the bathroom floor while waiting for Kenny to fall asleep on the couch. She had a stiff neck from the position she had lain her head on the edge of the bathtub. She listened for steady breathing, but heard nothing except for the occasional crack and pop of the dying fire. She eased herself from her sitting position and tried to stretch her neck. Kenny had left the bathroom light on and she didn't want it to wake him when she began her search. She took a few steps before realizing she would need to remove her boots to move silently over the hardwood floors of the cabin. She quickly removed her leather boots and stood in stocking feet to be able to soundlessly pad around the cabin. The pounding of her heart echoed in her ears as she flicked the light switch off to plunge the bathroom into total darkness.

April turned the knob and pushed the door slightly ajar, listening for any telltale creaks. There were none. She waited to move until her eyes adjusted to the semi-darkness of the living room and she could clearly make out Kenny's sleeping form bundled in a heavy blanket on the couch. The moonlight streaming in from the blinds that covered the windows helped her to navigate without walking into the furniture. She first went to his nightstand, then to his dresser. No keys. She next tried the kitchen counters, patting the countertops in the hope of feeling the familiar metal bundle. Still no keys. She went to the dining table and felt around it with her hands, then to the buffet against the wall. Nothing. April's heart sank as she remembered seeing Kenny put them in his front pocket when they first arrived. There was no way she could get the keys without waking him. A sob escaped as the tears came. She steeled herself against the feeling of hopelessness that threatened to envelope her. She couldn't stay trapped in here with Kenny. His earlier violent outburst, the way he pawed at her when she first came into the cabin. The man was a felon—a drug addict! He practically told her she was going to be raped. April knew she had made a foolish mistake. There was no way she'd marry Kenny Colt of her own free will. Her "man of God" was nothing but a bully and a liar, and certainly no Christian!

She had to think of another way to escape, but she still had to get the padlock off the front door. But how? April padded back into the kitchen and looked for a tool to break the padlock. In the dim streaks of moonlight, she managed to find the kitchen utensil drawer. As quietly as she could, she felt among the spoons and spatulas to see if there was something long and made of metal that could be used as a lever to break the lock. Nothing was heavy enough. She searched in vain for a tool chest.

She froze in her tracks as Kenny coughed. Had he awoken and observed her futile search? He coughed again. She scarcely dared to breathe as she waited, her heart pounding in her ears, as she heard the couch cushions groaning under his shifting weight. When it seemed an age since his last movement, April let her breath out. It was foolish to think she could find an easy way out of the cabin. She needed time and light to find the right tools. As the couch cushions moaned again, she decided what to do.

She stood still in the darkness until there was absolute silence, and then padded slowly to the corner of the fireplace. She would change into the clothes he had given her and pretend to be too sick to get out of bed in the morning. Then she'd have the day to herself. He had a computer, so there was a phone line in the house. A simple call to 911 would take care of everything. She smiled to herself as she slipped into the bathroom, silently closing the door behind her. As she felt the bathroom wall for the light switch, two strong arms grabbed her from behind as the lights blazed on. In the mirror's reflection she gasped as she saw Kenny's malevolent grin.

Dangling the keys in front of her eyes, he sneered, "Lookin' for these, darlin'?"

Chapter Thirteen

"What's the matter, baby? Cat got your tongue?" Kenny's sick laughter echoed in her ears and he squeezed her, hard. "No...uh, no. You startled me," April stammered. "I needed something for my stomach—and something for my head. I don't feel so good." She put her hand to her temple in an effort to emphasize her discomfort.

"Yeah, right. You're like all the others, April. Think you're too good for me, don't you?" He roughly pushed her into the vanity and her head smacked the medicine cabinet. He stood in the doorway and turned to face her. "Well, you're not going anywhere. You belong to me now, so get used to it. I can treat you like a queen or turn your life into a living hell. It's up to you. Now get out of those filthy clothes and put on what I gave you last night. Clean yourself up. You're disgusting!" His face was contorted with revulsion and April realized that he could barely force himself to touch her when she wasn't clean.

"Why did you poison me last night? You said you loved me." April slowly turned, resting her weight on her outstretched palms on the vanity. "If I'm disgusting, it's because of you, Kenny. You make me sick." She stood not two feet away from him and slowly closed the slight distance between them.

He took a step back, his rage mounting. "I told you to get yourself cleaned up! Then get in the kitchen and fix my breakfast." His words came out between clenched teeth. "You have fifteen minutes to be standin' in front of that stove." He stormed out of the bathroom. April rubbed the spot on her forehead that had hit the cabinet's wood frame. It already started to form a knot. In dismay, she saw that there wasn't any kind of lock on the bathroom door. There was no way to barricade herself in the tiny room until he left for work. Checking out her watch, she saw that precious moments had already passed. April turned on the water and found a washcloth and began cleaning her face. She wouldn't shower or wash her hair. Maybe that way he'd keep his distance. Once he was out of the house she would shower, after calling the police. In less than an hour this nightmare would be over. She allowed herself the first happy thought since coming into the cabin.

April pulled on the sweatpants and tee shirt that Kenny had left her. The pants were baggy but warm, while the top was loose with short-sleeves and she could feel her arms getting goose bumps in the chill of the morning.

She padded out of the bathroom, holding her filthy clothes from last night in her hand. "Where should I put these?" Kenny was adding wood to the fireplace.

"There's a clothes basket in the closet." Kenny didn't look up from working the logs with a poker and she could feel the heat spreading into the cold cabin. Fearful of triggering his anger, she went to the bedroom closet and put her clothes on top of the hamper. There were several flannel work shirts hanging in front of her and she pulled one from a hanger and put it on, covering her bare arms.

In the kitchen, she searched through the lower cabinets, looking for cookware. She found a couple of frying pans, and after setting them on the cook stove she went to the refrigerator and got out some bacon and eggs. She turned a gas burner on, and when it didn't ignite she shut it off and looked around for a box of matches. Glancing at her watch, she saw that it was 6:15 and her ordeal would be over in another 45 minutes. She would make Kenny a nice breakfast and send him off to work like a dutiful wife, make her escape, and then go...where? The thought struck her like a proverbial ton of bricks that she had nowhere to go. Kenny would drive off in her car. The only item she could see that was hers was the coffeemaker. Where had Kenny put all her other things that had been crammed into the Escort? Her apartment was gone. Her job was gone. All she had were her clothes from yesterday, her coat, her purse and the coffeemaker. Well, she'd leave it to the police to get everything back for her. She was mixing eggs in a bowl when Kenny came from behind and wrapped his arms around her. "You look pretty sexy wearin' my shirt, baby." He nuzzled her neck and held her in a warm hug. She was startled for a second and then resumed mixing the eggs in a bowl. "Whatcha' makin'? Sure smells good." He kissed her ear, sending shivers of revulsion through her.

"Scrambled eggs, bacon and toast. Sound okay?" She tried to sound cheerful as she shrugged out of his hold.

"I'd rather have you for breakfast, darlin'." He reached for her again as she stirred the eggs around in the pan.

She slapped playfully at his hand. "Now, Kenny, you can show me where the plates are or go set the table yourself. There's plenty of time for that when you get home tonight. Today I'll unpack my things, if you'll tell me where they are, and get myself settled in. When I'm done with the dishes I'll see what's in the freezer so I can make a special dinner for us. After all, this will be our first real night together. "

He turned her around to face him and held her by her shoulders, looking deeply into her eyes for a long moment. April smiled sweetly and he bent his head to kiss her. She fought her revulsion and forced herself to meet his lips with her own. She dropped the spatula and held him tightly. "I'm sorry I was such a problem last night. I'm feeling much better now. I'm here with you, exactly where I want to be." She looked into his eyes, her own wide with innocence, as she held him in a warm embrace.

"Now, baby, that's more like it!" Kenny bent to pick up the spatula and rinsed it off, dried it, and handed it back to April. "I'll set the table."

April finished buttering the toast and brought plates to the table. She sat down as Kenny took her hand in his and lowered his head. She kept her eyes open during the prayer, however. There was no way she was going to take a chance on being poisoned for a second time by this madman! He mumbled a blessing over the food and it was all she could do not to roll her eyes toward heaven. What a hypocrite!

April was as sweet as she could be when she sent Kenny off to work. She walked him to the door and watched as he took a brass key from his wallet and unlocked the padlock. He turned to face her, and after replacing the key said, "I hope you know that everything I do is for your own good, darlin'." He held her chin in his hand and kissed her goodbye for the third time. April genuinely smiled at him, thinking to herself that it would only be a few moments before she would be free. "I hate to leave you, but I've got to go to work. You know how it is. I love you, April."

"I love…" Kenny pulled the door shut behind him and she heard the padlock snap in place just inches from where she stood. April leaned against the heavy wooden door and sighed in relief. Her ordeal had come to an end! She rushed to the computer, looking for the telephone, and found it sitting atop his answering machine on one of the shelves. She grabbed the handset and put it to her ear, almost giggling in relief. As she reached for the keypad to dial 9-1-1, the phone went dead. She pressed "0" for operator several times, but there was no sound. April heard a noise outside the window and opened the blind. There, with his nose pressed flat to the glass, was a widely-grinning Kenny.

"Have a nice day, baby!" He shouted. He flung a snowball at the glass, turned and walked away. She watched him get inside her car and head down the driveway, slowing at the gate. April backed away from the window, letting the blind fall back in place. She sat down at the table with her head in her hands and wept uncontrollably.

By the time she was out of tears, she found a new determination to escape. She would find a way to get out of the cabin, locate the phone box on the outside of the house and somehow, someway, reconnect the line.

April knelt on the couch and opened the blind, securing it so it wouldn't get in her way as she climbed through. The windows were fairly new and had a typical-looking lock that she slid to one side with her fingers. So far, so good. Next she raised the window and opened it about eight inches before it completely stopped. She could feel the cold air seeping in, even though the storm window was securely in place. A careful inspection showed there were large nails hammered into both sides of the frame, allowing only the eight inches or so of the opening. She would have to find a hammer to remove the nails before she could open it wide enough to crawl through. She shut the window, deciding to get dressed for the outdoors, but she couldn't shake the feeling that she needed to hurry. She hoped Kenny had been honest about going to work, but how could she know if he was telling the truth? He made such a production of locking the front door, yet the windows were easily used for escape. Surely he knew she'd find a way out of her prison.

She wouldn't let herself be deterred from finding an escape. A feeling of uneasiness grew until it was almost overwhelming. In the bedroom closet she found an insulated flannel shirt to layer over the one she already wore. On a peg by the door hung a black knit cap. She twisted her hair into a knot and pulled the cap down securely over her head, covering her ears. She searched for tools in the kitchen, but there were none to be found. Afraid of wasting precious time in her search, she opted for a two-tined meat fork to pry the nails out of the window frames. She prayed its thin metal handle would hold up to the force she would need to use. She zipped her boots up, wishing she'd worn socks instead of pantyhose last night. April grabbed her coat from its peg and put it near her purse on the couch. Taking the meat fork and uttering a silent prayer, she worked the nails for several minutes each until they were loosened in the soft wood. First one clunk, then another, as each nail hit the hardwood floor and rolled under the couch. Adrenaline pulsing through her body, she shoved the window with all her strength, then the storm window. They both opened enough for her to easily climb through. She still wondered at Kenny's lack of securing the windows as she reached for her coat. She was straddling the window now, one leg out and one leg in, and tossed her coat through the window to land on the porch. As the second sleeve of her coat cleared the window sill and fell, she felt a sickening crunch as something grabbed the heel of her boot. Almost afraid to see what it was, April slowly turned her head, her eyes following the path of her coat sleeve. Horrified, she saw that she almost set her foot into the cruel, metal jaws of an animal trap.

She was shaking so badly she could scarcely force herself to move from her position on the window sill. She took several deep breaths and watched carefully where she stepped, slowly pulling herself completely out through the open window. Her knees felt like rubber bands as she tried to walk toward the other end of the porch and find the phone box. She managed to make her way down the front steps and found a stick big enough to set off the trap that was under the front window on the other side of the door. The ugly metal jaws flew several inches into the air with the force of their clamping shut. April shuddered to think that someone who had professed to love her could lay such unspeakable traps for anyone—animal or human. She hobbled on her broken boot heel to the side of the cabin and found the green plastic box she prayed was for the phone line.

Bending over it to get a better look, she lifted its hinged lid and sought out any wire that looked like it might be loose or disconnected. Her cold fingers weren't moving as nimbly as she would have liked and she blew on them, hoping for some warmth. As she stood up to wiggle her fingers and get the blood flowing, she saw a reflection in the window glass, moving so fast she didn't have time to react as she was lifted and forcefully body-slammed into the unrelenting log wall of the cabin. There wasn't enough air in her lungs to scream or moan as she slipped into unconsciousness.

Chapter Fourteen

A heavy boot pushed roughly into her side, rolling her over as she heard the distinctive click of a pistol being readied to fire.

"One stupid move, Colt, and you're a dead man. Get up slowly and keep your hands where I can see them."

April painfully struggled to her knees, losing her balance several times as she tried to keep her hands behind her head. Now what? A new terror arose in her as she realized that the deep, threatening voice behind her didn't belong to Kenny.

"Okay, now. Hands behind your back." April hesitated. She heard the rattle of what she imagined to be handcuffs. She'd rather be dead than handcuffed and at the mercy of another madman. She heard the crunching of crusty snow as heavy boots carried her assailant to within a foot of her trembling back.

"Hands behind your back! Now!" The order was given a second time, and a trembling April put a shaky left hand out to her side.

"Whoa...and what have we here?" As April slowly turned to face her attacker, he took the quivering hand and examined it. "April?" When he realized she was a woman, the big man returned his weapon to its holster inside his coat and the handcuffs disappeared.

April nodded and pulled her hand away from the stranger's. She turned very slowly, unable to control her shivering, her mind whirling inside her head. Under lowered lashes she looked up at a big, muscular man. He was over six feet tall, swarthy and good-looking. Big brown eyes returned her puzzled stare. With his dark mustache, April imagined that he could be mean-looking and intimidating when he needed to be.

"Patti sent me, April. She thought you might be in trouble." April leaned into the big man and couldn't stop her tears. He put his arms around her as she sobbed, smoothing her hair. "It's okay, now. I'm here to take you home." The big man whispered into her hair, comforting her as he would a child.

April wiped her tears with the flannel sleeve of Kenny's shirt and forced herself to stand on her own. "I'm sorry. I- I wasn't sure I was going to make it out of here—alive." She hicupped as she fought for composure. "My purse. I need my purse." She limped toward the front porch on her broken heel. Reaching the window she had used for escape she bent to pick up her coat, but the unmovable jaws of the trap held one sleeve in a death grip. She stammered at her rescuer, "He..he…I can't believe..." Her throat constricted as a new wave of tears threatened to overtake her.

"It's okay, sweetheart." The stranger tried to soothe her fears and coax her along at the same time. "Let me…"

"My name's April, not 'sweetheart.' Just April," she said, looking directly into his deep brown eyes. She turned and leaned into the window, pulling her purse from the couch. When she had retrieved her handbag, she tried to pull her coat free, but the steel jaws still held it tight. She dropped the coat with a loud *thunk* back onto the front porch, where the trap had almost claimed her leg. She found herself shivering uncontrollably, and still in a daze, limped down the porch steps and stood for a moment with her rescuer, looking back at the cabin where she'd been held prisoner overnight. "I'm ready."

Neither one spoke as they covered the distance from the cabin to the wooden gate at the end of the driveway. They were walking as fast as April's broken boot heel would go through the crusty snow. Her feet were numb from the cold and she almost fell when they reached the gate. Her rescuer led the way as they slipped next to an old oak tree and bent between two strands of barbed wire to reach the road. April struggled to keep pace with the man in front of her, her breath coming in smoky gasps in the frigid winter air. At last they rounded a corner and April saw a black Dodge Ram truck with a camper shell, looking as powerful as its owner, sitting off to one side on the wooded, country road. He unlocked the driver's door with a remote device on his keychain. He turned to April, picked her up by the waist and set her on the seat. "Hold on." He took her left leg and slid the sweatpants over her boot and gently removed the boot from her foot. Next he did the same with her right boot. Wincing from the sting in her cheeks as her face started to thaw, she drew in her breath at the intense pain she began to feel in her toes and feet. "You're gonna be in a world of hurt for about ten or fifteen minutes while your feet get warm. I'll be right back." He reached into the cab of the truck and slid his keys into the ignition, turning on the powerful engine, then reached to pull at a lever under the seat and went to the rear of the truck. April heard some rummaging around and slid her bottom, using her palms, onto the passenger side of the truck. Her feet were still on the driver's seat as he came around and stood in front of her, extracting two thick wool socks from his jacket pockets. April sucked in her breath from the pain in her toes as he lifted first one foot, then the other, and maneuvered the socks onto her frozen feet. He lifted them with one hand as he slid into the truck and laid her feet on his lap. "You okay?" he asked, wincing with sympathy pains for her. He slammed his door shut as April nodded, holding her breath until the throbbing turned into a million needles stabbing at her toes.

"Oh...my...gosh," she managed. "I'll be okay in a minute." She tried to smile at her rescuer through gritted teeth.

He threw back his head and laughed. "Yes, I believe you will." He reached forward and adjusted the heat controls as April felt the inside of the truck getting comfortably warm. She pulled up her knees and turned in her seat, placing her feet gingerly on the floor of the truck.

"Put on your seat belt. Could be a bumpy ride." April did as instructed and wiggled her toes, feeling the weight of his stare on her. She smiled up at him and stuck out her hand.

"You already know my name. What's yours?"

"Lindsay. Bob Lindsay" He laughed at her formal handshake and noticed that she had a nice firm grip for such a dainty, manicured hand. He smiled. "My friends call me 'Big, Bad, Bob'. " He grinned.

April laughed and turned to look at the road ahead. Bob put the truck in gear and the big Dodge's tires slowly covered their tracks back toward the cabin. As they came around the corner, April gasped as they saw her white Escort coming toward them, then make a sharp turn into the drive, stopping at the wooden gate they'd slipped around. Kenny jumped out of the car and ran to open the gate, waving absently to the passing vehicle.

Bob nonchalantly waved back, but kept the big truck moving. He could feel April's fear as they passed Kenny Colt and reached out his hand to pat her own. "It's okay, April. He can't hurt you anymore."

She gulped back tears as they continued on towards town. When she could speak without fear of tears she whispered, "Thank you for saving me."

Bob turned and smiled again, giving her hand another gentle, reassuring squeeze as they drove, without speaking, into town. They went past the restaurant where she and Kenny had had lunch for the first time and she marveled at how the past week seemed like a movie of someone else's life. Certainly not her own. She thanked God for her rescuer, and at least for the moment she felt safe and secure with this kind and powerful stranger.

They continued down Main Street and made a left onto Maple, heading toward the neat, red brick building that spanned half a block. Bob pulled the truck into a parking space near the front door of the Oakwood Police Department and told April to stay where she was. He came around and opened her door, waiting patiently, while she unfastened her seatbelt. She grabbed her handbag as he reached around her shoulders and under her knees, carrying her easily in his strong arms. She turned the lock and pushed the door closed. She wrapped her arms around his neck, whispering again, "Thank you, Bob. Make that 'Big, not-so-bad' Bob Lindsay." She smiled and snuggled into the collar of his jacket, and for the first time since coming to Oakwood, Missouri, she didn't feel afraid.

Chapter Fifteen

"This is ridiculous, deputy. April's been drugged, held against her will, nearly raped. And you're telling us there's nothing you can do?" Bob stopped his pacing long enough to stare the deputy straight in the eye, trying to keep his anger in check. Making an enemy of the deputy wouldn't help April's situation.

"Look here, Mr. Lindsay. She's given us no grounds to arrest Mr. Colt." The deputy held up one finger, then two, then three. He looked from Bob to April while he spoke. "She willingly gave the man her car keys and permission to drive her vehicle. She admits she willingly entered his home. If you want to take her to the hospital, maybe we can do something about her being drugged, but other than that, from a legal standpoint, Mr. Colt's done nothing wrong." Deputy Shipley shrugged his shoulders. "The only thing I can suggest would be for Miss Stover to file an *exparté* order at the Recorder's Office over at the courthouse."

"What's that?" April asked.

"A restraining order," Bob explained as he put a hand on April's shoulder. "It's up to you. What do you want to do?"

She looked at Bob and then asked the deputy, "Can someone come with us to pick up my car and things? My car's been unloaded and I didn't see any of my things inside the cabin. I don't own much, Officer, but it's all I have. Some of my clothes are at Pastor Wilson's house, too. I don't think a restraining order will help. I want to go home and never see that--that horrible man again."

"What sort of 'things'?" asked the deputy, readying his pencil.

"My computer and printer. My coffeemaker. Two boxes of books and notebooks. Clothing. Personal items. I--I can't think everything." April stammered, trying to remember exactly what her worldly possessions amounted to. "It all fit in the trunk and back seat of my car, so it wasn't much." She looked hopefully at the young man who sat at the desk in his uniform of dark brown shirt and mud-colored slacks. "I have a bag at the Wilson's with my clothes and makeup...blow dryer...curling iron." She shrugged again, wondering what the two men thought of her meager collection of earthly goods. She felt very small and inconsequential. As the tears started to well up in her eyes, Bob stopped his pacing and stood directly behind her, gently kneading her shoulders. Her feeling of being all alone evaporated and she felt her courage returning.

"Let me go talk to the sheriff and see what we can do." Officer Shipley pushed back his chair and stood, taking the report he'd made of April's ordeal with him. "Why don't you two get a cup of coffee? Right through that door." He pointed to a door with a little glass window in the center of it. "I'll be back shortly."

Bob reached his hand out to April and she took it. They walked to the metal door and he swung it open, letting her precede him into the break room. He shoved his hand in his pants pocket, searching for change.

"Oh, no you don't!" April piped up. "The *least* I can do is buy you a cup of coffee!" She had her wallet ready and slipped some quarters into a coffee machine. "Black? Cappuccino? Since you saved my life, I think cappuccinos are in order."

He laughed and walked to one of three empty tables in the small room. Pulling out a chair, he took a seat and watched this woman. This funny-looking, remarkable woman, he thought to himself as he pulled on his moustache. He had easily mistaken her for a man in the outfit she was wearing. Stray strands of dark hair had fallen from under a black knit cap, a loose plaid flannel shirt over baggy black sweats with tan wool socks completed the outfit. April carefully took a few steps to the table, watching the liquid as it swished in the Styrofoam cups, careful not to spill any. "Here you go." She set one cup in front of Bob and sat down opposite him, taking a tentative sip before putting her wallet back in her purse and zipping her handbag closed.

"You okay?" he asked with genuine concern. Dark circles were under her eyes, her cheeks pale; her lips the palest pink. He wondered what she would look like on a typical day. "I know this must be hard for you."

"I'm more worried about what you and Patti and Max are thinking about me right now." April mumbled her answer, watching the steam rise from her cappuccino in an attempt to avoid those deep, questioning eyes. The thought of being pitied filled her with as much dread as the thought of being ridiculed.

"Patti and Max think you're pretty special and I think you're pretty lucky to have friends like them." He took a sip from his cup.

"Yeah, I am." She nodded. "I feel like such a jerk. Patti tried to talk sense into me, but I wouldn't listen. I wanted so badly for Kenny to be all that he said he was." She looked at Bob, a questioning look on her face, trying to gauge his opinion of her by his facial expressions. She noticed that he had the quirky habit of pulling on his moustache. Maybe it was to distract anyone from reading his thoughts.

His eyes met hers and he chuckled. "You're not the only one that's made bad choices, April. If you knew some of the stupid things I've done over women in my life--well, it doesn't matter now. We've all made mistakes." He shook his head, staring into his cup, some old memories being laid to rest.

She smiled to herself, liking the little crinkles at the corners of his eyes when he laughed. He was a kind man. She was grateful he hadn't made her feel like a fool. She could handle that all by herself.

Deputy Shipley pushed through the door as April and Bob swallowed the last of their hot drinks. "Sheriff says to follow you in the squad car and make sure Colt doesn't start any trouble. You ready?"

"Ready as we'll ever be." Bob rose from the table. He took April's elbow as they left the break room. She shuddered involuntarily at the thought of having to face Kenny again. Bob saw the look of reluctance and fear shadow April's features and put a comforting arm around her shoulders as they exited the police station.

He unlocked the truck door and helped April climb into the passenger seat. He handed her the keys, saying "Start her up while I figure out the plan with the deputy, okay?" She forced a smile and slid over to the driver's side.

"Okay." Her chest heaved with a heavy sigh as he walked away. She watched his long-legged, easy stride as he went to the squad car. Bending over, he leaned over the deputy's open window and April could see their frosty breath cloud as they spoke together. Bob nodded his head and headed back to the truck.

He slid easily into the seat and blew into his cupped hands a few times before putting the truck into reverse, then backed out of the parking space. "Gettin' cold out there." He put the Dodge in drive and followed the police car. "First we're going to drive past the shop to see if your car's there. If not, we're going to the Wilson's to pick up your clothes. Then we'll go to the cabin." He looked at her out of the corner of his eye. She was staring straight ahead, trying to be brave. "You okay?"

"Yes... I'm fine. I--I hate the thought of seeing any of those people again. Kenny told the pastor lies about me. Told him I was a drunk. But I couldn't stand and talk straight last night because he'd poisoned me." April was trembling with the frightening memories of last night's ordeal, clasping and unclasping her hands.

"You mean the pastor was at the cabin last night?" April nodded her head. "He did nothing to get you out of there?" Bob was incredulous that she could have been helped hours ago. No wonder she didn't want to face these people. "That's some pastor, April. And these people—the Wilsons? They've known him for a while?" She nodded again and watched him shake his head in disbelief.

The ride to the Wilson's was soon over and they rounded a corner and April saw the now-familiar house and driveway. Bob pulled alongside the squad car as April saw Marian's stern face peering out from behind the kitchen curtains. The curtains dropped back into place as Deputy Shipley picked up the mic from his car radio and spoke a few words, then put it back in its dashboard holder and got out of the squad car.

"You ready?" Bob didn't blame April for her reluctance. "We'll take your things and go. Ten minutes from now this will all be a memory." His hand squeezed hers and she marveled that this stranger could make her feel so safe with no more than a reassuring touch. With Bob at her side, she could face the Wilsons and Kenny Colt with a strength she had never known before.

"Thank you, Bob." She squeezed his hand in reply. "I'm ready." She scooted toward him as he got out and picked her up as he had earlier when he carried her into the police station. Still clad in his wool socks, April had no shoes on her feet. She wrapped her arms tightly around Bob's neck and tried to look as dignified as possible as he carried her up the back steps. The pastor opened the door and stood back, flanked by Marian, as the deputy, Bob, and April entered the kitchen.

"Is she still drunk?" barked the pastor. "I won't have her in that condition in front of Marian!"

"I was never drunk!" April sputtered. "Kenny drugged me. I begged you for help and you turned your back on me!" Tears welled up in her eyes again as she struggled to gain control of her emotions. "Marian, I..." The emotions won as April lost control and started crying, hiding her face in her hands. Marian came around the kitchen table and put her arms around the distraught young woman.

"It's okay, April. Pastor knows that Kenny can twist a tale around to suit his own needs, don't you, Pastor?" Marian's unexpected kindness made April sob even harder as she returned the older woman's hug. "Come in the bedroom and let the men talk for a moment." As Marian started to lead April toward her temporary bedroom, Bob stopped them.

"Are you okay with that, April?" He took her hand in his and squeezed it. April nodded and walked down the hall with Marian, wiping her tears on her sleeve. She could feel Bob's eyes on her back as the distance between them grew.

Marian sat on the edge of the bed and motioned for April to sit down beside her. She put her arm around April's shoulders and tried to think of the right words to soothe and comfort her. "Kenny's got some serious problems, April. I wanted to warn you from the first moment I saw you, but Pastor insisted I keep out of it. It wasn't my business to interfere with your relationship. Now I wish I had said *something*." Marian sighed and took a hankie out of her dress sleeve, wiping April's tears. "Now, you go take a shower and get out of those awful clothes. I'll make us all a pot of coffee." She stood to leave, hesitated, then turned back toward April. "The good Lord really *does* work in mysterious ways, April. You have to trust Him that the right thing has happened here."

April nodded and sniffed a few times. Her heart felt heavy with sadness and her chest heaved as she stood to rummage through her suitcase for a pair of jeans and a warm top. She was mortified as she glimpsed herself in the mirror. She looked hideous! She'd forgotten that she still had on Kenny's knit cap and clothes. Bob had been talking to her all morning and she looked like...like... She couldn't find the words. She now felt totally humiliated. Bob and the police must think she was really a piece of work! She grabbed her makeup bag and clothes and ran to the bathroom in the hall, purposely not making eye contact with anyone, although she knew Bob was watching her every move.

"Wow!" Bob stood as April entered the kitchen, a big smile spreading across his face. Instead of the ragamuffin he had rescued earlier, a beautiful young woman stood before him. Long, silky dark hair framed her face, and in her jeans and top there was no mistaking that she was all woman. Beautiful expressive eyes looked directly into his own, as he pulled a chair out for her at the table. "You look much better. How are you feeling?" She laid her bag on the floor next to the wall, set her purse and heavy, dark pink sweater on top of it.

"I *feel* much better, thank you." April blushed and smiled as she noticed the appreciative looks she got from both Bob and Deputy Shipley. Marian busied herself with pouring April a cup of coffee and setting a plate of pastries in front of the famished girl. "Thanks, Marian. I haven't eaten in quite a while." April chose one of Marian's muffins and halved it, smoothing butter on both sides. "Marian makes the best blueberry muffins I've ever had," she said, popping a piece in her mouth and washing it down with hot coffee. April devoured two of the delicious muffins and had a second cup of coffee while those around her discussed how best to approach Kenny Colt.

"Well, April, if you're about ready, I think it's time we got your things from the cabin. Pastor Wilson's coming with us.

We'd like you stay here with Mrs. Wilson, but you're the only one that can identify your property." Turning to face her, Bob had taken April's hand. "Okay?"

She pressed his hand in both of hers, so grateful for her kind rescuer. She almost wished that she didn't have her car. She would miss the comfort of having Bob next to her during the long ride back to Patti and Max's house. "Thank you, Bob. I don't know what I would have done without you. I hate the thought of going back to the cabin, but I want to get this over with."

"I'll get your bag." He handed April the heavy sweater that was lying on top of the bag. She pulled it over her head, smoothed her hair, and felt Bob's eyes on her again. She knew the dark pink knit was a good color on her and she was happy that Bob seemed so pleased at her transformation.

The little group marched down the steps to the vehicles after April hugged Marian goodbye and thanked her for her kindness. Pastor Wilson walked with Deputy Shipley to the police car and got in on the passenger side, while Bob and April went to the black Dodge. He unlocked the passenger-side door and looked at her for a long moment. "I'm going to miss carrying you around." She smiled and reached her arms around his neck as he picked her up, his strong hands encircling her small waist, and set her on the seat. Shutting the door and walking around to the driver's side, he got in and turned the key in the ignition. They backed out of the Wilson's driveway and waited until Deputy Shipley pulled out ahead of them, his bubbles atop the patrol car silently whirling blue and red lights.

They wound around the hills and hollows, April seeing the road in daylight for the first time. As they neared the wooden gate, April's heart picked up its pace and her pulse quickened at the memory of last night. Her adrenaline was surging as she readied herself for whatever stunt Kenny would pull this time.

She took a couple of deep breaths to steady herself as they watched the deputy open the gate and return to his vehicle. The police car pulled through the gate and into the cabin's parking area and they followed behind, watching the deputy and Pastor Wilson get out of the car. Bob pulled the Dodge forward a bit and then backed in, turning the truck around, facing the gate, lining it up with April's Ford.

"It's showtime."

Chapter Sixteen

April stood mostly hidden behind Bob's solid body when Kenny opened the heavy wooden door. She watched a parade of emotions cross his face as he looked at each of the men standing in front of him. When his eyes met hers, there was no mistaking the raw hatred and fury directed at her. He quickly turned his attention as Pastor Wilson began to speak.

The pastor removed his hat and held it in his hand. "This gentleman and Deputy Shipley have come for April's things, Kenny."

"Come in, Pastor. I only just got the place warm again." Kenny smirked and stood aside, motioning for the group to enter. Bob stepped between April and Kenny as they entered, keeping an arm around her for support, while directing a menacing stare at April's captor. He could feel her stiffen, even under the thick jacket he wore. "Instead of calling me at work to let me know she was leaving the place to freeze solid, I guess she thought she'd make her point by letting my pipes freeze. Nice, huh?"

April averted her eyes from Kenny, but she observed the differences between him and Bob. Besides the obvious physical differences, Kenny was whining like a child. She couldn't believe there had ever been any attraction to him, never mind actually considering marriage.

"Miss Stover says you forcibly kept her against her will, that you drugged her and kept her a prisoner overnight. Is that right, Mr. Colt?" Deputy Shipley accused Kenny in his most official manner. April moved away from the safety of Bob's protective arm as she walked past the group and went to the kitchen and unplugged her coffeemaker. When she returned, she smiled to herself as she noted the intimidating stance that Bob had taken—feet apart, hips slightly forward, arms crossed over his chest. His head lowered a bit as he kept constant eye contact with Kenny under thick, dark brows. He looked positively menacing! If April hadn't come to know his gentleness over the past few hours she would have been worried for her life. She was certain Kenny was worrying now, even with the presence of the deputy. "I'm wondering if any of this violates your parole? What do you think, Mr. Colt?" Kenny's head jolted to look at the deputy.

"She's a liar! She was drunk and acting like a slut in here last night. I didn't do anything to her. Ask Pastor! He was here!" Kenny shouted in desperation, pointing to Pastor Wilson. Bob shifted his weight and Kenny grew silent, seething anger from every pore as the pastor looked down at the hat he held in his hands.

"Where's her stuff, Mr. Colt? I think Miss Stover will agree not to press charges if you return her property right now."

April walked back to the group, holding her coffeemaker and its glass pot carefully, making sure the pot didn't fall to the floor and shatter.

"Her *crap's* out in the shed, but I'm going with you to make sure she doesn't take anything that isn't hers, *the lying slut*." He threw on his coat and pulled the keychain out of his pocket, choosing a small padlock key. He led the way through the front door, turning left on the porch, passing the window where April had almost lost her leg. She shivered as she hurried by, wondering where the traps were now.

Thirty feet behind the cabin was a small log shed with a fresh path of footprints made through the snow. Kenny pulled its doors open and stood back. The smell of kerosene spiked the air in the small enclosure. April walked to the stone steps and entered the small room, seeing her boxed belongings stacked in a pile to the left. On top of the stack was her winter coat, shredded to bits.

"My coat! You couldn't kill me, so you took it out on my coat?" she cried in disbelief. "I can't believe it. Leave it here. I don't want anything he's touched." April shook her head and then pointed to the small stack of boxes. "Those are mine, deputy."

"I need her car keys." Bob towered in front of Kenny.

"Get 'em yourself." Kenny flung the keys into the snow and then stood on them, his hands on his hips, defying Bob's order. The deputy walked into the shed with April, as Bob easily knocked a surprised Kenny down and retrieved the key chain.

"You'll pay for that!" Kenny seethed. "You'll *both* pay for that."

The pastor went to Kenny, offering a hand. "Let it go, Kenny. You need to calm down. Give April her things and let her go." The pastor huddled with Kenny in the snow, trying to distract his furious parishioner, as Bob walked to the Escort, carrying several of the cardboard cartons.

"April, come here," Bob called. April and the deputy carried the rest of the boxes and set them behind the car. Bob set his cartons alongside the cherished coffeemaker inside the trunk, and had removed the packing tape from one. April noticed duct tape now securing her boxes, but she had used transparent sealing tape when readying them. "See if there's anything you can salvage in this one," he said in disgust. April leaned over the trunk and saw what Bob was referring to. Kenny had opened her boxes and poured kerosene on her belongings. Her books were ruined! She ripped the duct tape from the next box. Kerosene had been poured inside the box containing cookbooks and linens, too. April stood, staring, feeling her throat tighten as she gulped back her tears. Had he destroyed everything she held dear? The third box revealed her photo albums. Streaks of kerosene ran through them as well, but most of the pictures could probably be salvaged. The computer was spared, but the box had been tampered with. The box containing her printer and other computer accessories only seemed to have been rifled through. The boxes containing her clothing were beyond help. Greasy stains of kerosene soaked all the way through. No amount of detergent would be able to remove the odor.

"You're a monster, Kenny Colt!" April sobbed, picking through her ruined clothes, the tears streaming down her cheeks. "I can't believe what an idiot I was to have ever believed that you were a religious man! God talked to *you*? It sure wasn't the same God everyone else believes in! How can you be so hateful?" Bob held her close for a moment and glared at the grinning Kenny Colt. Kenny forced a loud laugh and mimicked April's words. The man was obviously in need of psychological help and Bob doubted the pastor had the credentials for the kind of help Kenny needed. Bob whispered in April's ear. She still sobbed, but tried her best to stem the flow of tears, then walked back to the cabin.

"Get out of my house!" shrieked Kenny, running toward the cabin. The deputy and pastor ran after him, while Bob quietly tossed the ruined boxes of clothing from the car. He unlocked the Escort's front door and leaned inside, shifting the car into neutral, then secured the Escort to the tow bar he had taken from the back of his truck. After he was satisfied the car was securely fastened to the truck, he joined the others in the cabin.

As he climbed the front porch steps, Bob could see April, framed in the bathroom's doorway, unmoving. She finished washing the kerosene from her hands as Bob had instructed her to do.

"*You*! *You get out!*" Kenny screamed as he turned to see Bob entering the cabin. "You take this whore and both of you get out before I *kill* you!"

Bob's eyes searched April's as he asked, "Are you okay?" April nodded, her eyes wide and flinching with every curse that spewed from Kenny's rant, scarcely two feet away. Bob walked past the deputy and the pastor as he made his way to April's side, his hands raised. "Let me wash up and we'll be on our way, okay?" April nodded again and sighed in relief, despite the tension in the small cabin. She was certain the pastor had never seen Kenny act so foolishly, although the deputy didn't appear overly concerned, undoubtedly having been witness to countless domestic disputes during the course of his career. Kenny continued to threaten Bob and April as they descended the front porch steps, but he made no sudden moves toward either of them. Bob took April's elbow as they made their way to the front of the truck and he unlocked the passenger door. She stood and put up her arms up to encircle Bob's neck as he picked her up again by her waist and set her down on the seat. April didn't know what had overcome her, whether it was the urge to hurt Kenny, or if it was an act of gratefulness that overwhelmed her, but she closed her eyes, pursed her lips and pulled Bob close. She felt a split second of hesitation before his lips melted into hers, and for a moment she forgot all about Kenny Colt.

When they finally pulled apart from the kiss, Bob slowly cocked his head to one side and smiled gently at April. "I don't know where that came from, but I'd sure like another one before the day's over." He held her trembling chin in his hand for a second as they made eye contact and smiled at each other, ignoring Kenny's nonstop verbal assault. As she was sinking into the dark brown pools of his eyes, Bob tore his gaze away and took Kenny's key chain out of his pocket. "Lock the door." He handed her the truck keys and took her chin in his hand once more, barely touching her lips with his own. "Another minute and this will all be history. I'll be right back."

April watched Bob in the side mirror as he took long-legged strides back to the men at the porch. He spoke with the deputy

for a moment and handed Kenny's ring of keys to Officer
Shipley. He then shook hands with the deputy and the pastor.
April smiled as her rescuer slid in beside her. "Are you ready to
make this place history?" He smiled. She nodded, blushing
slightly at her earlier boldness with big, bad Bob. "Slide on
over next to me, April. We've got company." He reached out
his arm to put around her, watched his mirror and stepped on
the gas at the same time. The Dodge inched forward and she
felt the pull of the Escort as it followed behind. Bob kept his
foot steady on the gas pedal as he headed toward the gate. They
were about to clear the gatepost when Kenny jumped on the
truck's step and pounded his fist on April's window, his nose
flat against the glass. April gasped and cringed closer to Bob's
warm body as Kenny jumped back to the ground, his words
coming in loud and clear.

"*I'll get you for this, you tramp. You're both gonna pay!*"
She could see his arm punching the air in anger, his mouth
blowing frosty storm clouds of chilly air.

"Thank God it's over," she whispered. "It's finally over." She
cuddled next to Bob and closed her eyes, trying to erase the
events of the past week from her memory.

Chapter Seventeen

They put two hours' worth of miles between them and the small town of Oakwood when the sun started to set in the western sky, a blazing orange ball surrounded by deep purple haze. Bob pulled the Dodge and its cargo off the highway into a little strip mall that had several different stores, restaurants and a motel. April had slept during the last several miles, exhaustion finally overtaking her. When the truck came to a stop she instinctively jolted upright, the comforting hum of tires on pavement no longer lulling her into sleep.

She smiled through heavy-lidded eyes at Bob, who was watching her as he released his seatbelt. "I think we need some dinner and a good night's sleep." He brushed the hair from her eyes. "Are you hungry?"

"I'm famished," April mumbled, freeing herself from her seatbelt and reaching down to get her purse from the floorboards. "Let me run a brush through my hair."

She dug around in her purse and then flipped down the sun visor to use the mirror and gave her hair a few quick strokes. She applied lipstick and made an air kiss at the mirror, then turned to Bob with a big smile on her face. "Okay, I'm ready!" Bob laughed as he exited the vehicle and came to April's side. They walked arm in arm to the front door of the restaurant and were greeted with a display case that showed off artfully decorated cakes and pies. The smells wafting from the kitchen made their mouths water in anticipation of a wonderful meal. A smiling young waitress rattled off the dinner specials as they followed her to a red vinyl booth. After removing their coats, Bob and April slid into the cozy booth across from each other and got comfortable. Bob ordered a beer, and April a glass of wine. They read their menus, each very much aware of the other's presence, each uncertain as to what would happen between them next.

April took a sip of wine. "I really want to thank you, Bob. I don't know what I would have done without you." She glanced at the man in front of her and suddenly felt shy.

"I'm glad I was able to help. I don't really understand why you went to Oakwood, though. Do you mind telling me about it?" Bob pulled thoughtfully on his moustache, watching April study the glass in her hand. She was blushing a bit and he guessed it was more from the events of the past week than from the effects of the wine.

"I guess he showed up when I was lonely. He flattered me and I fell for it." April tucked a piece of hair behind her ear, not looking up.

"You met him at the bookstore?"

"Oh, no. It's much worse than that," April said, more to her wineglass than to Bob. "I met him on the Internet. After a while I gave him my phone number and we started talking. He sounded like he really cared about me. He told me over and over about being a Christian and how God had touched his heart." She looked to see if Bob was laughing at her. "I--I really feel stupid…telling you this." Her hands continued to play with the stem of the glass and she wouldn't make eye contact with him again. "It—sounds so desperate."

"April. April, look at me." Bob slid his hands across the table and covered April's with his own. "I don't think you're stupid or desperate. I think you're brave to travel this far for something you believed in." He was still talking to the top of her head. "If he turned out to be the kind of man he said he was, you would have had a happy life with him. This isn't your fault."

April looked into deep brown eyes and saw only concern, not ridicule.

"Ready to order? Or should I give you lovebirds a little longer?" The waitress winked at April and grinned broadly at them both. April pulled away from Bob's warm hands and smiled awkwardly as she reached for the menu.
"I think we'll both have a couple of steaks, baked potato, salad." Bob said to the waitress. To April, "Or are you one of those no fat, no frills kind of gals?"
"Make mine medium rare." She grinned at him, snapping the menu closed and handing it back to the waitress. Bob ordered them each another drink and the waitress scurried off, picking up plates from another table across the room.
"What about you?" April asked after taking another sip of her wine. "How do you know Patti and Max? And how is it you happened to be available to rescue me?"
Bob mocked a hurt expression. "I can't believe Patti hasn't bragged on her infamous cousin, 'Big,bad Bob.' I thought I had a bigger reputation than that!" He grabbed at his heart, shook his head and laughed. April smiled and felt herself relax in the company of this warm, caring man. The waitress came to the table and set two bowls of fresh colorful salads in front of them, followed by a loaf of bread on a little wooden board with its own knife and a dish of soft butter. She smiled and said their steaks would be out shortly, then moved on to the next table.
Bob and April ate in companionable silence for a few moments, remarking on how good the salad dressing was, how crisp and warm the bread. When the steaks came, they held off on serious conversation until they were full and satisfied, finding it easy and comfortable to be in each other's company. Too full for dessert, they ordered coffees to take with them to the motel and made the short walk to the single-story row of rooms that stood to the west of the parking lot. The sputtering red neon light illuminated the entrance to the motel's office and Bob opened the door, letting April enter first. An old couple sat

behind the counter, their eyes glued to the television set that blared the theme music from a popular game show.

"Got one room left with a double bed. Will that do ya'?" asked the old man, still not looking up from the television.

Bob and April exchanged a glance. "That'll be fine." Bob said as a card and pen were set on the counter in front of him. He filled out the information and slapped his credit card on the counter. The old man automatically ran the card through a slot on a machine that spit out two receipts, slapped Bob's card back on the counter and handed the receipts to Bob for his signature.

"Keep the yella' copy, young feller." A large gold key with a bright red plastic octagon, the number eight written with black magic marker, was then laid on the counter. "Number 8." The old man still hadn't taken his eyes off the television in the corner and the old woman hadn't as much as spared them a look either.

As the door closed behind them, April and Bob laughed hysterically. "I've never seen anything like that! They didn't even look at us; that must be *some* show!" Arms around each other, they giggled all the way to the door that had a gold "8" in the middle of the front panel. April held the coffee as Bob slid the key into the lock. He felt on the wall until he touched a light switch and the black void that had greeted them lit up to reveal a quaint, cozy little bedroom. Pine paneling with flowered prints on the walls gave the room a homey feeling. There was a double bed to their right, with a night stand on each side, a dresser with a television set on top, flanked by two matching chairs to their left. Straight ahead was a mirrored hallway that revealed a closet to one side, a tiny bathroom to the other. It was sparsely furnished, but immaculate.

"Oh, I'd love to have a hot bath," April sighed. "With lots of bubbles."

"Why don't you run your bath while I get our gear? I'll be right back."

April set coffee on each night stand and lay her handbag on the bed, wondering about their sleeping arrangement. She was drawn to Bob's kindness and his good looks, but she wasn't ready for anything so intimate. She hoped he wasn't expecting some kind of sexual repayment for her rescue, even though the thought of spending the night with him sent a guilty thrill through her. Three knocks on the door brought her out of her daydream. She opened the door and took her bag. His cheeks were rosy from the chilly night air, his eyes bright and wide. April was drawn to him, watching his movements as he took off his jacket and set his own bag on one side of the bed. "Am I okay over here, or is this your side?" He smiled at her.

"No, you're fine." She smiled back. "I--I'll go run my bath now." She took her bag into the bathroom and got the tub ready with her favorite bubble bath. She wrestled with the thought of locking the bathroom door. If Bob heard the click of the lock, would he think she didn't trust him? She decided to leave it unlocked as she wound her hair into a knot and pinned it to the top of her head. Once settled comfortably under the blanket of suds, she wasn't worried about him walking in on her. She relaxed, then shut her eyes, the musky, floral scent of the bubble bath mixing with the heat of the water, the comfortable feeling of a full stomach and the security of being with Bob all worked together to lull her into a happy slumber.

A knock on the bathroom door startled April awake as she realized that she'd fallen asleep in the tub. Bob peered around the corner. "Are you okay?" His worried expression made her laugh.

"I'm fine. I must have dozed off. Sorry." April shivered, the water temperature having dropped in the last half hour. Luckily, her blanket of suds was still pretty much intact. Bob smiled and entered the bathroom. He put down the toilet seat cover and sat down, a big grin on his face.

"You're kinda cute with your hair up like that," he said. Without taking his eyes off her face, he could see her starting to color. "I never knew a blush started so far down on the body either."

"Bob!" April squeaked, sliding lower under the water and the cover of the suds.

"Here, turn around and I'll wash your back." He unfolded a white washcloth that was stacked on the bathroom's vanity and found a tiny bar of soap. With some difficulty, he got the wrapper off and dipped the bar into the water. "Whoa, that's pretty chilly. Want some more hot water?" He turned the hot water on again as April nodded and then rolled over in the water and leaned on her forearms. He rubbed the bar of soap on the washcloth a few times and then got on his knees beside the tub. The water temperature was heating quickly, and so was his own. He gently rubbed April's back with the soapy cloth and then used his hand to scoop clear water and run it down her back. "I don't suppose you want anything else washed, do you?"

"Bob!" she squeaked again. He laughed and leaned over to kiss the middle of her shoulder blades, then stood, unfolding himself to his full height.

"I'm sure glad you didn't marry that guy, April." She turned her head and saw that he was serious and looking at her with a mixture of emotions. He was tender, yet businesslike at the same time. When the door closed behind him, April rolled right side-up in the tub.

"So am I, Bob. So am I," she whispered. When she was dry and in her nightgown she stood in front of the bathroom mirror and went through her nightly ritual that ended with brushing her teeth. Another light knock on the door and it slowly opened to reveal Bob, his eyebrows raised in a question. She bent over to rinse her mouth in the sink. "I'm done now. Bathroom's all yours." She smiled. She turned toward him and saw that he wore only his jeans. He was carrying a clean tee shirt and pajama bottoms in one arm and with the other he reached for her and pulled the pin that held her hair. He watched as her hair cascaded down her shoulders to frame her face.

"Beautiful." He put his hand on the back of her head and pulled her toward him. She put out her hands and felt the strength of his chest, his powerful muscles moving under smooth skin as he dropped his clothes on the vanity and pulled her into an embrace she didn't resist. She leaned her head back and welcomed his kiss. Her heart pounded at the wild thoughts going through her mind. She pulled away and smoothed her hair with her hands.

"Wow, Bob, I--I." She placed her bag between them.

"Yeah, me too." He said and let out a loud sigh. "Go on, now. Outta here!"

April laughed as she padded to the double bed and looked to see what shows were on the television. She folded the pillow on her side of the bed in half and climbed in under the covers, pulling them up to her chin. The pillow had her head at an awkward angle, but at least she could see the screen. The television did no good, though; she couldn't stop the thoughts of Bob racing through her mind. How could she be so attracted to a man she barely knew? A week ago it was Kenny who had filled her thoughts every waking hour. Granted, he'd betrayed her trust. He'd lied to her, drugged her and turned violent. But was it possible to put emotions so quickly in her past? Her heart raced, thinking of Bob. Big, bad Bob! She smiled at the thought of those three words describing the man in the bathroom. Yes, he was big, but there was nothing bad about him. He was kind and caring and generous. Literally, her knight in shining armor. He came to her rescue and she couldn't help but love him for that alone. It seemed that there was something special between them in the few short hours they'd known each other. April didn't want it to end. She didn't know a thing about him, except that he was Patti's cousin and he'd saved her life.

The water stopped running and April could hear him moving about the bathroom. She imagined him standing with only a towel wrapped around his middle. He would be in bed with her in a moment, and she felt her heart pounding at the thought. The bathroom door opened as Bob padded toward the other side of the double bed. He wore his pajama bottoms and tee shirt, which did nothing to hide the muscles of his chest and flat stomach. April sucked in her breath when she looked at him. He went to the door and checked the lock, then shut off the overhead light, leaving only the television for illumination. He climbed into bed and leaned over her for a moment and kissed her lightly on the lips. She smiled at him, but made no move to lower the covers. He lay back down on his side. "Good night, sweetheart," he said. She rolled away, mumbling her goodnight. He scooped her back towards him, fitting her backside to his front, like two spoons fitted comfortably together. April froze, loving the feel of him around her, yet afraid of too much happening too soon. She realized a few moments later that she had nothing to fear from Bob...his breathing, deep and regular, let her know that he was fast asleep.

Chapter Eighteen

April awoke to the sounds of highway traffic rushing by and Bob's deep bass voice competing with the water hitting the plastic shower curtain. Her lips parted in a smile, remembering the times she'd woken during the night and felt his protective arms around her, the comforting weight of his body next to hers. She leisurely stretched and glanced at her watch, wondering how much time they had left together. By the end of the day they'd be at Patti and Max's. Would Bob continue on, out of April's life, or would he wait until she sorted through her experience with Kenny and was ready for a loving relationship? She wondered about the women in his past. Surely there had been women. He was handsome and charming, after all. What was not to love? April decided to make the most of the time she had left with him and live in the moment, not dwelling on the past nor worrying about their future.

The water stopped and a few minutes later the bathroom door swung open. Bob came around the corner, grinning at her.

"Good morning, beautiful! Hope I didn't wake you."

"Good morning, handsome!" April shot back. She reached for him as he came to her side of the bed and leaned down for a kiss. "I think I woke up when I realized it was cold in here without you." She laughed. He kissed her a second time before he grabbed the motel room key and stuffed it into his pocket.

"I think I'll call Patti from the restaurant and get some coffee while you get ready, then we'll eat breakfast and get on our way. Sound good?" He stood back from the bed and packed his things into his duffel bag, zipping it shut.

April watched him, reminding herself that she wasn't going to think past the moment they were in. "Okay. I'll hurry and get in the shower. Coffee sounds wonderful." She smiled at him, committing to memory every detail of his face, his hands, the way he moved. She scooted off the bed and rummaged through her bag to find another favorite top, needing to look her very best today. It would either be his last memory of her—or the first day of the rest of their lives together. She smiled as she hoped for the latter, trying to push thoughts of any future from her mind.

The floor was cold on her bare feet as she padded into the bathroom to brush her teeth, then started the shower, making sure the temperature was comfortable before stepping under the spray. She let the warm pressure wash away all the awkwardness and horror of the past week, thanking God that Patti had sent Bob to rescue her from a terrible mistake. She finished washing and rinsing and stepped out of the shower, wiping the foggy mirror, then quickly dried herself in the rapidly cooling air. She heard the door open and close, then voices from the television. She hummed as she blow dried her hair, eager to finish her primping so she could spend as much time as possible in Bob's company. She put the finishing touches on her makeup and gathered her personal items in her arms, leaving the bathroom.

He'd opened the curtains wide while she was in the shower and April saw him silhouetted in the bright light that shone from the plate glass window. Her heart leapt with happiness at the now-familiar sight of him pulling on his moustache, lost in thought. She hoped he was thinking of her.

Her bag was on top of the bed and she quickly tucked away her things, zipping it closed. April looked up to see his intent gaze focused on her. She colored slightly, not used to being stared at by a handsome man. Her heart raced as he smiled devilishly at her and announced, "I think I've got some really good news for you, April."

"You do?" Her eyebrows arched as she eagerly awaited his next sentence. He sat and smiled at her. "Well...tell me! What is it?"

He laughed at her frustration and took a long and infuriatingly slow sip from his coffee cup. "Patti found you another apartment." He wiggled his eyebrows at her and smiled again. "It's partially furnished, closer to the bookstore, same amount of rent..." another deliberate and tortuous drink of his coffee... "*and* she said the landlord's a good friend of hers. I'm to bring you straight there and they'll meet us at seven tonight, with pizza, to celebrate our return."

April let out a squeal of delight and ran to Bob, giving him a bear hug. "Oh, Bob! I can't believe it! That means she's forgiven me! I still have my job!" Tears of happiness welled up in her eyes. "I get to have my life back!" She straightened and hugged her chest as Bob took the lid off another Styrofoam cup and handed it to her. They toasted coffee cups to her good fortune. Bob congratulated her, while April beamed with joy. "I can't believe she found me another apartment. Patti's something else, isn't she?" April shook her head in wonder at the kindness of Patti and Max, not to mention Patti's handsome cousin, big, bad Bob.

"Coffee's cold already." Bob made a face, draining the cup and tossing it into a small wastebasket. He stood and reached for April again, holding her. "It's great to see you so happy, April."

"And it's all *your* fault," she teased. "Now let's eat before I starve to death. Happiness makes me hungry. I can hardly wait for that pizza tonight!" She reluctantly pushed herself away from his cozy embrace and got her purse, while Bob deposited their bags in the back of his truck. They met on the sidewalk and put their arms around each other as they walked to the same restaurant where they'd eaten last night.

"Well, if it isn't my favorite lovebirds," smiled the same waitress who had served them steak dinners the night before. "Coffee, right?" April blushed and looked up at Bob under lowered lashes. He was watching her, and he smiled. When she finally lifted her head, he laughed and patted her hand.

They nodded and chatted with the pleasant waitress for a moment as Bob decided on the "Truckers' Breakfast Specials" for them. They flirted a bit over coffee and April's eyes grew wide when the plates were set before them. Mounded over with pancakes, eggs, toast, sausage and bacon, the tempting smell made her realize how hungry she was. They stopped talking long enough to polish off their breakfasts and have a second cup of coffee.

"Good thing I like a woman with a hearty appetite." Bob leaned back in the booth, laughing with her once again. "Can you cook?"

April grinned. "I guess you'll have to come for dinner and find out for yourself."

"I'd like that, April. Very much." Their eyes locked for a long, solemn moment, their hands reaching for each other across the table, until the waitress jarred them into reality, dropping the check in front of Bob's plate and gathering the dirty dishes.

"Y'all come back now, lovebirds!" She giggled and disappeared behind swinging doors that led to the kitchen.

The humming of the tires on pavement made a pleasant background noise to their conversation in the following hours. April told Bob the details of her life that had led to her meeting with Kenny. Then it was Bob's turn. April wanted to hear it all. He told her of his huge family, what it was like growing up with parents, brothers and sisters, cousins, aunts, uncles, grandparents. To April it sounded like a wonderful dream, nothing that remotely reminded her of her own childhood. He told her of the trouble he'd gotten into as a boy with his cousins and brothers. Fishing and camping out. His brief marriage to a girl that grew bored, waiting for him when he'd joined the army. His hitchhiking cross-country to see America and the numerous jobs he'd held along the way. How he liked animals and people. He told it all, with joy and laughter. The more he spoke lovingly of his family, the more April wanted to be a part of his life—a very special part of his life. She silently reminded herself that Kenny had sounded wonderful too, but Kenny had wanted her to exclude everyone else in her life. Bob wanted to share his family with her. Kenny was in a rush to claim her; Bob hadn't even suggested a date yet, although she prayed that he would. They seemed to fit together so effortlessly and naturally. She'd only known him a little more than a day, but already she didn't want to think of being parted from him. In her musings, she grew quiet.

"Everything okay?" he asked her, taking his eyes off the road momentarily.

"I'm trying to picture your family, and wondering what the apartment will be like. What to make for dinner the night you come over." She laughed.

They settled into an easy camaraderie, stopping for lunch an hour or so from home.

"I'm having such a good time with you that, in a way...well, I don't want you to disappear out of my life," April admitted over her Chef's Salad, anxious for his response.

"I've enjoyed your company too." Bob put down his fork and reached for her hand. "Let's get you settled in and see if you still feel the same way once you're safe in your old routine."

"Why wouldn't I feel the same?" April cocked her head and looked into the deep brown pools of his eyes that she could sp easily get lost in.

"Well…" He paused, choosing his words carefully. "I've helped you out of a tight spot and you're grateful to me for that, but once the routine of daily life sets in, you might decide that I'm a pretty boring guy. We had one heck of an adventure. The rest is downhill. You haven't had a chance to mourn the death of your relationship with Kenny. I want you to be sure that it's me you really want."

"Bob, I'd never think of you as boring. You're the kindest man I've ever known. And, yes, I'm grateful that you rescued me. I can't believe you'd think that I might change my feelings for you."

His strong hands squeezed hers gently. "April, I've been through this before, helping a lady out of a jam. There's something about the danger that draws people together and makes you think you're in love—or something close to it. But when the day to day living kicks in, things change. I'll be off on a case and you'll get tired of waiting and then I'll be history."

"What exactly do you do? What kind of 'case'?" April gulped and felt her throat tightening, tears welling in her eyes.

"I do different kinds of work. I have a Private Investigator's license, a few years background in law enforcement, martial arts training, and I hold a gun permit. Being a 'jack-of- all-trades' gets me some interesting work. Bodyguard, bounty hunter, courier. Even bringing Patti's best friend back home." Bob smiled and tried to keep his tone light, but he could see that April thought he was brushing her off.

"I see." April pulled her hands away, her appetite gone. How could she have been so foolish as to think he'd been interested in her? He was a nice guy, doing his job. April swallowed back her tears and forced a smile on her face. "I'm sure you're right." She dabbed at the corners of her mouth with her napkin, crumpled it and tossed it on her plate. "I'm ready when you are."

Bob tried making small talk for the remaining hour of their drive home, but April's spirit had been crushed. The worst of it was that he was right. She had yet to deal with the feelings she'd had and then lost for Kenny. She would never know how she truly felt if she jumped into a relationship with Bob. Big, bad, handsome Bob. She couldn't think straight with him so close to her. She wanted so badly to be in his arms that she literally ached for him. It was easier to distance herself emotionally; physically was a whole different story.

April dealt with mixed emotions as they turned off the highway and onto the main road that would take them straight through town. They started passing the landmarks she knew so well—Jensen's Dairy Farm, the state park entrance, the tractor repair. Two blocks from town, near Patti's bookstore, Bob put on his blinker and pulled smoothly in front one of the town's older buildings. "Here we are, right on time. It's the corner apartment. You're on the second floor." The bottom floor was vacant and its windows covered with newspaper, but April could see light shining from the bare windows in her new apartment.

"It's great. And so close to work. I won't have to do much driving." April tried to sound happy. "Thank you, Bob. You've been really great." From the corner of her eye she saw movement and turned away from him at the instant he was reaching for her. There were Patti and Max, rushing to open the door for them. Max hugged her so hard she felt like a squished kitten, held too tightly by a small child. Patti pushed Max out the way and the two women laughed and cried together on the sidewalk. As Patti fired off questions and April answered, Bob and Max freed April's Escort from the tow bar and drove the car around the alley behind the building, Max getting details of the story of April's rescue from Bob.

Patti opened a small door from the front sidewalk that went to a narrow stairway. On the little mailbox attached to the doorframe, Patti had already inserted "Stover" in the name slot. So this was it. April caught Patti's enthusiasm, and her spirits rose. They climbed the stairs. Patti made April cover her eyes as she led her into her new apartment. After several steps, April lowered her hands and gasped. It was perfect! Hardwood floors and eggshell walls. A built-in bookcase. "Patti, I love it! It's gorgeous!" They walked through the living room into the kitchen. Lots of cabinet space. New appliances. A dishwasher! Down the little hallway was a full bathroom, clean and bright. A linen closet at the end of the hall and a good-sized bedroom with a huge walk-in closet completed the apartment. April was thrilled. She'd never had such a nice place before.

The men entered the apartment through the back door in the kitchen, Bob carrying April's bag. Max toted one of the computer boxes and set it down on the counter.

"Where do you want the computer? Living room or bedroom?" Max asked.

"Oh, gosh. I don't know. I'm overwhelmed with this beautiful apartment! I think the bedroom closet for now. After I get some furniture, I'll decide." The men went back out for the rest of April's boxes.

Patti and April busied themselves with paper plates, paper cups and napkins. "Well, what do you think?" Patti asked, grinning broadly at April.

"I think that I'm lucky you care about me," April said seriously. "I think I would have been dead if you hadn't sent Bob to find me." She gulped her emotions back down, remembering the comfort of being held in Bob's strong arms.

"Not that, silly! Of course I care about you. What do you think about Bob?" Patti opened the lids on the two pizza boxes, filling the room with the mouth-watering smell of one of April's favorite foods. "Isn't he terrific?"

"He saved my life, Patti. I think he's wonderful," April muttered, taking ice cubes from a bag in the kitchen sink and dropping them into paper cups. She poured soda into the four cups that were neatly arranged in front of her.

"That's *it*? No sparks?" Patti stood, dumbfounded, in front of April, her hands on her hips and looked her square in the eye, waiting for a detailed response. "Well?"

Bob and Max chose that moment to come in with in the rest of April's belongings. April felt the heat of Bob's stare on her. She looked quickly away, breaking eye contact with the man who had stolen her heart and then thrown it back at her. Patti gave her a questioning stare, but said nothing, as they all converged on the pizza boxes.

They sat on the kitchen floor and ate as April told of her ordeal. The conversation then focused on the new apartment and what plans April had to decorate it. When did she want to start work at the bookstore?

When Patti and Max got ready to go, April noted that Bob made no attempt to leave with them. She rose and walked with her dearest friends to the back door and they exchanged hugs once again. At the top of the stairs, Patti insisted that April should come for coffee at the bookstore in the morning, and April agreed. She stood at the top of the stairs, waving, as Max and Patti got into their car and drove off. She watched until the taillights disappeared around a corner, then breathed a deep sigh, almost afraid to find out why Bob had stayed behind. She turned and looked into the eyes of the man she'd come to love. She hesitated a moment before stepping back into the kitchen. Pulling the door closed behind her, he swept her up in his arms and held her close to his heart, whispering in her ear, "I'm not leaving until we get this settled."

Chapter Nineteen

"There's nothing to settle, Bob. You were doing your job and I'm very grateful. I got carried away with my feelings." April pushed away from his embrace, turning her head as the tears welled up again.

"Look at me." He gently took her chin in his hand and turned her face toward his own. "April, this has been the most miserable few hours of my life. I didn't mean to hurt you. I was afraid of that same stupid speech from you, so I said it first." Her eyes remained closed, a lone tear trailing down her cheek. "April, I've been falling in love with you since I first tackled you back at the cabin. You're beautiful and brave and funny. I want to be with you, but I want to make sure that's what you want too."

April slowly opened her eyes. "You're...falling in love with...with me?" she whispered. He nodded and tickled her nose with his moustache in the sweetest kiss April could ever remember. The weight that had hung heavy on her heart shattered into a million pieces and she wasn't sure she could feel the ground beneath her feet.

They sat together on the linoleum floor and talked until April could barely keep her eyes open. Bob went out to his truck and brought in a sleeping bag for the night. He smoothed it out on the bedroom floor while she got ready for bed, brushing her teeth and hair.

He had turned out all the lights in the apartment except for the bedroom and kitchen by the time she came out of the bathroom. April walked him to the front door and they stood holding each other for another eternity, making plans to see each other the next afternoon. When they kissed goodnight for the final time, April stood at the top of the stairs and watched his every move—those long legs taking the stairs reluctantly. He turned at the bottom step and said a husky "I love you, April," then he slipped out the door to the street. She locked the door and stood at the window, watching as the truck's headlights turned on and she heard the rumble of the engine as it hummed to life. After sitting for a moment the Dodge slowly pulled away and the taillights disappeared from view.

April practically floated to her bedroom, feeling enveloped in Bob's love. She never experienced this range of emotion with Kenny or anyone else she had ever cared about. Bob's love made her feel beautiful and alive and strong—giddy and silly at the same time. She twirled around her new bedroom, hugging herself, and felt certain she wouldn't be able to sleep with all the thoughts churning through her mind, but the moment she slid into the sleeping bag and could smell his familiar scent, she drifted off into a deep, peaceful sleep.

In the morning she awoke as soon as the first rays of the sun caressed her face. She lay still, blinking her eyes for a moment, remembering that she was in her new apartment. Her lips slowly parted in a lazy smile as she imagined herself back in Bob's warm embrace. Forcing herself to move, she stood back from the windows and watched the town come to life from her second-story window. Today would be a busy day. Before Bob returned this afternoon she would meet with Patti, find out about starting back to work, and look for furniture. She needed new clothes, too, since Kenny had poured kerosene on most of her belongings. She had to sort through her things and see what needed replacing. In a way, she was starting a new life and all the changes would be for the good. She wasn't the same person that had left this town a week ago. As the image of Bob's smiling face broke into her thoughts, she took her last clean pair of jeans, top and underclothes into the bathroom to shower and change.

Soaping her hair, she made a mental list of all she needed to accomplish over the next couple of days. Her new apartment came with a stove and refrigerator--an empty refrigerator. The kitchen cabinets needed to be stocked. She owned a computer and a bag of dirty clothes, but that was about it. It would take a lot of shopping to fill her new apartment and closet. Luckily, she lived frugally and hadn't transferred a dime of her savings into Kenny's accounts, as he had insisted she do immediately after their wedding. Her ill-fated trip hadn't cost much, either: two tanks of gas. She rarely used her credit card, so furnishing her new home wouldn't be a problem. She felt special and blessed, despite all that had happened, and she hummed a tune as she readied for the short walk to the bookstore. It was going to be a great day! The first day of the rest of her life!

Chapter Twenty

His anger intensified with each slushy step. All other thoughts evaporated from his mind there was only her. Each step reminded him over and over that she had rejected him sexually and then humiliated him in front of the pastor, the deputy and that other guy. And who was that other guy? She had no family, so the whore must have had another boyfriend. Well, nobody treated Kenny Colt like that and got away with it. She belonged to him. He would find her and punish her. He would teach her a lesson she'd never forget.

He took no notice of the cold. The rage that boiled inside him drove him with a relentless fury. She was nothing but a tramp. After all he'd done for her, she took off with that man. Took the car that should have been his. Her money was supposed to be deposited into their joint account. She didn't do that either. He was out the money and the wheels. The woman lied to him and stole from him. Kenny stopped in his march down the wooded road as a thought hit him like a thunderbolt. It was the pastor's fault! If the pastor hadn't kept them apart when she first got here she wouldn't have found that other guy to take her away.

The pastor's house came into view as Kenny rounded the last corner of the country road in quick, angry steps. The full moon silhouetted the house and garage almost as clearly as if it were daylight. Kenny's boots crunched on the snow as he walked to the garage and pulled the door up. It opened easily and Kenny walked around the big hulk of the Buick to the driver's door and pulled on the handle. It opened easily and he slid into the driver's seat, adjusting it to his own shorter legs. He moved the rear view mirror a bit and adjusted the side one as well. Kenny bet the gas tank was full. If nothing else, the pastor was meticulous and always prepared. Now all he needed was the car keys.

Kenny marched up the steps to the kitchen door and twisted the door knob in his hand. It, too, opened easily. Kenny laughed out loud as he entered the kitchen. The pastor was such a trusting fool. He stood for a moment, waiting for his eyes to adjust to the darkness. The car keys dangled from their hook by the door. Kenny snorted in disgust at the lack of security in the pastor's home. The old man deserved what he got for being so damned stupid. Kenny marched through the living room and into the bedroom of the sleeping couple.

"Pastor!" Kenny shouted, kicking the dresser. "Pastor! Marian! *Wake up*!" He could hear their startled gasps as they realized that someone was in their bedroom. "*I said wake up!*" Kenny screamed at the top of his lungs. He flicked on the overhead light and saw a startled and teary-eyed Marian, sitting up straight, a pillow held across the front of her chest. The pastor whispered a fervent prayer as he reached for his wife. He finally blinked his eyes open, and with something close to relief, realized who was standing in front of him.

"What's wrong, Kenny?" he asked in concern, trying to sit up. "What's happened?"

"*You're* the one that caused April to run off with that guy. It's your damn fault she left me! I'm going to get her. I need your car." Kenny stood in the doorframe, his chest heaving, adrenaline oozing out of his pores.

"Calm down, son," the pastor said as he sat on the side of the bed. "Let's talk this out." He gathered his bathrobe and tied it around his waist as he padded toward Kenny. "Let's let Marian get back to sleep." The pastor pulled the bedroom door closed behind him, giving Marian a sideways glance toward the phone, hoping that she would understand.

Kenny paced back and forth in the kitchen like a madman. The pastor saw the crazed look in the younger man's eyes as he continued to berate and curse the older man. Kenny paused in his tirade as he saw the red light on the digital phone in the kitchen begin to blink. Marian! Kenny ran to the bedroom and flung the door open, grabbing the handheld phone from her trembling hand. He brought the handset down repeatedly on her head as she tried to fend off his blows with her thin arms. "No!" The pastor came in and tried to pull the madman away from his wife. It did no good. Kenny's viciousness was on automatic pilot as he pummeled away at the man who had been his friend. When neither the pastor nor Marian had the strength to fight back, Kenny dropped the handset to the floor and marched into the kitchen. In the bottom drawer of one of the kitchen cabinets he found a roll of packing tape. He went back to the bedroom and roughly pushed Marian on her belly and pulled her arms behind her back. He wound the tape around her wrists several times and rolled her over on her back again. He did the same with the pastor. Next he took the packing tape and bound their ankles together. He finally ripped off a piece and smoothed his hand over the tape on their mouths, partially covering their noses.

That should keep them quiet for a while--long enough to take care of business with April and her buddies. Kenny ripped the phone plug out of the wall before pulling the covers up and over the pastor and his wife. They deserved a nice long rest, the traitors! He flicked the light switch off and closed the bedroom door behind him. He walked back to the kitchen and replaced the roll of packing tape in the drawer at the bottom of the cabinet. Turning off the kitchen light, he grabbed the car keys from the hook by the door and pulled the door closed behind him.

The full moon was a stark light in the black of the night sky. Kenny tried to find "the man in the moon," but couldn't. No matter, he thought as he opened the door to the Buick and slid into the driver's seat. He backed the car out onto the country road and put the car in "park." Climbing out, he walked back to the garage and pulled the door closed, leaving the place as he'd found it. Well, almost. Kenny laughed hysterically for a moment and got back into the car. Yep, he was right again. A full tank of gas. Pedal to the metal and he was on his way to teach that evil Jezebel of a woman a lesson she'd never forget.

Chapter Twenty-One

Patti had been watching the front door since 8 a.m., eagerly awaiting April's arrival. When she spotted her friend crossing the street to the shop, she ran out to greet her on the sidewalk. "I thought you'd never get here! Coffee's on. Come on, come on!"

"What are you so excited about?" April giggled as she let herself be pulled along through the store. She stopped in her tracks and grabbed Patti by the shoulders, suddenly serious. "Patti, thank you so much for sending Bob to me. You saved my life. I was a total idiot and I'm so sorry for the grief I caused you and Max. Can you ever forgive me?"

"Are you done?" Patti in turn held April by the shoulders and tried to look stern. "It's over and done with. That creep ought to be in jail. We're thrilled you're back." She took two mugs and filled them with April's special brew of coffee. "I don't even want to talk about that jerk. He's history. I want to know if you're going to start back here on Monday." Patti put their cups on the table, "And I want to know what's going on between you and Bob!"

"You think something's going on between us?" April asked innocently, while her pulse rate soared at the mere mention of his name.

"Are you kidding? When he called yesterday morning he was on cloud nine. But last night you barely spoke to him. Now don't make me beg. *Pul-eeze* tell me what's going on." Patti sat on the edge of her seat, not wanting to miss a detail.

April couldn't hold her feelings inside any longer. Her smile broke into a full grin and soon the two women were giggling over Bob's good qualities, when the first customers of the day arrived. Patti was thrilled that her matchmaking efforts had worked and she was teasing April about "tying the knot" when

the phone rang. It was starting to get busy and April was eager
to furnish her new apartment. April finished the last of her
coffee and waved goodbye to Patti, who was ringing up a
customer. "I'll be back later!" she called out. Patti made a face,
but waved her out of the shop as a new group of book lovers
entered the store.

April walked the few blocks to the furniture store, with a new
spring in her step. The winter day was chilly but exhilarating,
and the sun seemed to smile down upon her as she greeted
everyone she met on the sidewalk with a happy "Hello." She
realized that she owed her new sense of self and well-being to
"big, bad Bob." His love had changed her life in miraculous
ways, and their relationship had barely even begun. She was
eager to test out her homemaking skills and had already
visualized her new nest--warm, cozy and inviting—when she
stepped through the front doors of Main Street Furniture. It
took her less than an hour to choose a comfortable living room
set, a simple oak bedroom suite, oak kitchen table and chairs,
and yes, they could deliver this afternoon! She took swatches
of her sofa and love seat fabric to the bed and bath shop, where
she purchased curtains for her new home, along with two sets of
linens with matching comforters for the bedroom. She chose
peach as the color for her bathroom accessories and enjoyed
choosing the shower curtain, towels, and bathroom rugs.

April returned to the bookstore around noon, dragging two
huge bags with her. Patti finished waiting on a customer and
ran over to help her weary friend. "Oh, my gosh! Did you buy
out Butler's Bed and Bath?" She laughed. April showed Patti
the fabric swatch from the couch and her new linens. Her
selections met with Patti's approval.

"The furniture's being delivered at 4. Patti, I could kiss you. I
love that apartment. It's going to be so beautiful and homey
when I'm done." April rattled on in excitement and Patti

116

laughed at her friend's new found joy, "oohing" and "aahing" at the appropriate times. In all their excitement the two women realized that they had missed lunch. The customers started to dwindle after one o'clock, so April called in an order to the sub shop. She agreed to stay and watch the store while Patti took the short walk to pick up their order.

April meandered among the bookshelves, searching for any new releases of her favorite authors. Her collection of books had been senselessly ruined by a psychopath. She shuddered at the thought, flashbacks of his outrageous behavior in her mind's eye, when the phone rang, bringing her back to the moment. She ran to the front counter and reached over. "Good afternoon, Rows of Prose." She could hear the sound of a television in the background, but no one spoke. "Hello? Hello!" She put the wireless phone back on its charger and hurried to open the door as Patti came in, her arms full of bags. The women carried their lunch to the back and sat at a table, the front door in view, as they spread their subs and chips in front of them and talked excitedly about Bob, April's new apartment and furnishings, and more talk about Bob as they picked at their food. The phone rang, interrupting their "girl talk," and Patti went to retrieve the phone.

"Yes, she's right here eating her lunch. Just a moment, please." Patti shrugged her shoulders and handed the phone to April.

"Hello?" There was no answer. "Hello? Is anyone there?" April was ready to push the "end" button on the phone when she heard her name. She brought the phone back to her ear, shaking her head and making a face at Patti.

"Yes?"

"You made a fool outta me. *I'll bet you're laughin' about me right now.*" April gasped, her eyes widening in fear. Patti leaned near the handset so both women could listen in on the phone call. "Well, you betrayed me and now you're going to pay, you slut! *After I kill your boyfriend I'm coming for you and that interfering friend of yours!*" The slow, deliberate words had accelerated into terrible screaming. Patti grabbed the handset and shut off the phone.

"Oh, no! Patti, what am I going to do? He's threatened to kill us all."

"Let's see if we can find out where that call came from." Patti pressed "talk" and dialed the operator. "Hello, I had a call I need to have traced. Can you help me?"

"I was afraid of that." Patti said, after putting the phone back down. "Unless he was on long enough to trace, we'll never know. Should we call the police, or talk to Max and Bob first?"

April paced back and forth for a few minutes, trying to remain as calm as possible. "I wish I knew, Patti. Unless he followed us back here, he can't know where I live. And I never told him where you live. I don't think he knows your last name, either. He has called me at work before because I gave him the number. It probably would be easy to find the bookstore, but..." April stopped in her tracks. "He doesn't have a car, Patti! He has no way to get here." She slapped the top of her head with her palm. "He's bluffing, Patti, trying to scare me again." April calmed down after she reasoned out the situation. She had discovered firsthand that Kenny was a master of manipulation. April wished she felt as confident as she sounded. He was frightening her now and she wasn't going to put up with it any longer. "When Bob comes over tonight I'll talk to him about it. I know Kenny's bluffing, but I don't think he should be able to do this and get away with it. Maybe I should have pressed charges against him when I was in Oakwood." She continued pacing, as Patti waited on another customer. April went to the front counter after clearing up their table from lunch. "Patti, I'm going back to the apartment. I need to be there anyway for the furniture delivery guys. I need to use your phone for one more call. I haven't had time to order phone service yet." Patti handed April the phone book.

"Here you go. Once you've got a phone you'll feel safer, too. Kenny's always given me the creeps. Car or no car, I don't trust him. Make sure you get an unlisted number, okay?" April smiled and dialed the number for the phone company, while Patti rang up another sale and chatted with her customer for a moment. April hung up and breathed a huge sigh of relief.

She waited until Patti rang up her next customer's sale and they were alone for a few minutes before planning her next few days. "Listen, Patti, maybe you and Max should come over tonight. How about eight o'clock? We can talk everything over with Bob and Max then. The installers will hook me up on Tuesday morning, so I'll be incommunicado for a couple of days. Tomorrow I'll finish my shopping for the apartment and groceries and set up my computer. I'll use Monday to finish getting the apartment straightened up and come over here for lunch. As soon as the phone's hooked up on Tuesday I'll give you a call. I should be able to start working again on Tuesday afternoon. What do you think?" April's eyebrows were raised expectantly for an answer. Patti stood there, shaking her head.

"Do you know how confident you sound? April, you're a new person since your experience. I'm so proud of you!" Patti hugged April tightly and gave her a "thumb's up". "What is it they say now? You go, girl!" The women laughed as April gathered her bags and headed out the door. "See you later!"

April walked to the alley that ran behind her apartment. Her car was parked neatly to the side of the back steps, leaving plenty of room for the furniture delivery van. She hoped the men would be able to carry the couch and dressers up the wooden stairs without any problem. She awkwardly half-carried and half-dragged the bulky bags, filled with her morning purchases. She dropped her bags as she entered the kitchen and quickly closed and locked the door behind her.

She couldn't shake the creepy feeling she'd had since Kenny's phone call. Why hadn't she seen how unstable he was long before she had uprooted her life and gone to him? How many others had he tricked this way, or was she the only gullible fool? A shiver went through her, even though she remembered what she told Patti earlier--he didn't have a vehicle to track her down, so he couldn't possibly carry out his threats.

April's musings returned to her fearless rescue by Bob and a smile formed on her lips. The love-of-her-life would be here in a few hours and she needed to start making her apartment into a home. She would force Kenny from her mind until she was safe with Bob and Patti and Max. Until then, she would happily daydream about big, bad Bob.

April busied herself with her purchases. She took the drapes and laid them flat on the carpeting, hoping they would smooth out on their own. She did the same with the kitchen and bedroom curtains. Next, she unfolded the peach shower curtain and hung it on its rod. She brought her "bed in a bag" linen sets in the bedroom and tried to decide which pattern she liked better. Both patterns were appealing, so she would ask Patti's opinion later tonight. Her mind switched gears to what to make when Bob came for dinner. She wanted their first homemade meal to be absolutely perfect, just as she wanted the apartment to be an appealing and perfect home.

Loud banging at the back door brought her back to reality as she hurried down the hallway. She reached for the dead bolt's knob and started to unlock it, as she peered out the back door window. Her heart skipped a beat. She was staring at the back of Kenny's head as he turned to face her.

Chapter Twenty-Two

"Ma'am? Ma'am, are you all right?"

"Oh, my gosh! I'm so sorry--I, I thought you were someone else," April stammered at the young man standing on her back stoop. "Oh, gosh! You frightened me!" She patted at her chest, trying to calm her heart at the unexpected scare.

"Sorry, lady. We're a little early with your furniture delivery. You are Ms. Stover?" asked the boy, holding a clipboard with a yellow receipt clipped neatly to the top, her name clearly visible.

"Yes. April Stover." She stood back from the door. "Please. Come in." The young man turned to wave to his companion who was still sitting in the truck marked "Main Street Furniture" across its broad side. The other man waved back and went around to the rear of the truck. April heard it being opened as she walked through the apartment with the young man, who really bore no resemblance to Kenny Colt other than height and hair color.

"Looks like your rooms are a good size to maneuver around in. I don't think we'll have any trouble with the couch or entertainment center. We'll go ahead and get started. Tell us where you want things." She met the men carrying her mattress at the kitchen door and smiled meekly, her heart rate slowing to normal. She tried to busy herself while they unloaded her new belongings, picking up the curtains she had earlier laid flat on the carpeting, and draped them over the shower rod in the bathroom. It didn't take long before the men were finished and April hovered, watching them remove the plastic from her mattress and box spring. She pulled out a bed skirt and asked them to wait a moment as she smoothed it over the box spring. Her mattress was set on top. She had them move the dressers around twice, and was grateful for the workmen's pleasant dispositions. The living room furniture wasn't set up quite like April had in mind, but she would rearrange it later, when she could really get a "feel" for the place. She apologized for not having anything to offer in the way of refreshments as the men assembled the kitchen set. She had them center it underneath the hanging lamp and she smiled as she looked around, pleased with the progress that had been made in so short a time. As the men left she gave each of them a twenty-dollar bill, thanking them for their hard work.

Alone again and locked securely in her lovely new home, she took the coffeemaker out of its box in the closet. She deliberated a few moments on where to set her favorite appliance, then plugged it in to the right of the sink. She poured a full pot of water into the belly of the Bunn and plugged it in. There was still plenty of time to go to the grocery store and pick up the basics. By the time she returned, the coffeemaker would be ready with a heated reservoir. Once the aroma of a fresh pot of her special brew wafted through the apartment, then April would feel at home.

She gathered her purse and hoped she could memorize all the items she would need for the next several days. To be certain the apartment would be free from intruders she tried the front door again. It was securely locked.

April took the back steps to her car. She couldn't reach the gas or brake pedals until she adjusted the car seat and mirrors so she could comfortably drive. She felt an involuntary shiver as she thought of Kenny driving her car as if it were his own. The thought of the man no longer angered or disgusted—the thought of him literally made her sick. She couldn't believe she had fallen for someone so selfish and cruel. She forced her thoughts back to the present and turned the key in the ignition. The Escort was as dependable as ever, starting right up. She took a right onto Main Street and drove the half mile or so to the grocery store. It felt like her lucky day as she slid into a parking space in the front row.

April was in high spirits again as she piled her cart full of food and drinks and all the necessities a new home would require. By the time she had finished walking every aisle in the supermarket another hour had passed and her thoughts had happily turned to Bob. She would soon be with him again and in his arms. She practically danced through the checkout.

The bag boy made small talk as he helped April out to the car with her cart full of bags. She unlocked the trunk and it swung open as she took the heavy bag the clerk was holding out to her. They were still chatting as a loud whoosh and metal snap startled them both. April touched off another of Kenny's animal traps with the weight of her grocery bag. Missing her fingers by a hairbreadth, the ugly jaws had ripped through the bag of frozen food. She stood dumb-founded, staring at the trap, then up at the clerk's face and back at the trap.

"Whoa, lady. That woulda' hurt *bad*! You okay?" the teenager asked. "You got any more of them in there?" April shook her head, still unable to speak. He cautiously peered into the trunk to see if any other traps were waiting in the dark interior. "Nope, just the one."

April's knees turned to rubber and she sank onto the Escort's bumper. "Oh, my gosh. I can't believe this." She shook herself back to the present. "Could you please take that thing and throw it in the trash can for me?" The boy gingerly picked it up, half of a frozen chicken still grasped in its teeth. He held the trap by its chain and walked it to the metal can outside the front doors and let it drop. April found a bill in her wallet and gave it to the young man. "Thank you. Could you please finish loading the groceries while I catch my breath?" He nodded and set her bags in the trunk, then closed the lid as April stood by and watched.

"Have a nice day, lady." He tucked the bill into his pants pocket and then turned to wave. "Come back soon." He whistled as he walked back to into the store.

Chapter Twenty-Three

April toted the last of the groceries up the stairs and set what was left of her frozen food in the kitchen sink. She hurried to lock the door, standing on the stoop for a moment to search the alleyway for any signs of life. Satisfied that no one was there, she turned the deadbolt and jiggled the doorknob to make sure she was safe inside. She couldn't shake the feeling that she was being watched, and she couldn't tell if it was from her latest scare, or if somehow Kenny had followed her to her new home. She checked the front door, making certain it was still securely locked. She stood to one side of the living room window and searched the sidewalks across the street, looking for anyone suspicious. It was getting dark now, and she needed to get her drapes and curtains up before nightfall set in. She seemed to be safe so she went to the kitchen and sat for a moment at the table, taking several deep breaths in an effort to calm her nerves.

Feeling a bit more relaxed, she put the cold items into the refrigerator and then filled the sink with hot water while she rummaged through the remaining grocery bags for the cleaning items she had purchased. April kicked off her shoes and brought one of the chairs over to the counter and, using it as a step ladder, washed out her kitchen cabinets. She did the same to the lower cabinets and drawers, frequently checking her watch, counting down the minutes as she waited for Bob. She brought the box from the bedroom closet that held pots, pans and other kitchenware and arranged her cupboards after meticulously washing the items from her boxes, not trusting that Kenny hadn't booby-trapped or poured poison over her few remaining possessions.

By 6:30, April had finished cleaning the kitchen and putting the groceries away. She took the last of her bags into the bathroom, cleaning the medicine cabinet and vanity drawers and stored away her soap, shampoo, and tissue. On her bed, she emptied her traveling bag and took makeup, curling iron and blow dryer into the bathroom and stored them in the linen closet. She then washed her face and freshened her makeup. A spritz of cologne and she was ready for Bob's arrival.

April padded into the kitchen to start a pot of coffee. She lit a new vanilla-scented candle and set it in the center of the coffee table, which was centered in front of the cozy couch. She located her favorite mug and a spoon, and stirred milk and sugar into her coffee and padded back to the couch, putting her feet on the coffee table. Sitting in the darkened room with only the cozy flame of the candle for company she took a long, slow sip of the sweet elixir and assured herself that everything was going to be all right.

She heard the opening and closing of a distant door and realized that someone was coming up the front stairs to her apartment. With her back against the doorframe, she cautiously turned her head and peeked out the window. She saw Bob's truck in the dim lamplight, parked on the street directly below her apartment. He rapped lightly as she turned the locks and opened the door, her joy evident at his arrival.

"Hello, beautiful!" Bob's face lit up when he saw her smile. He held one arm behind and with the other, took April by the waist and drew her close. She responded, wrapping her arms around his neck and savoring the warmth and feel of his lips, giggling as his moustache tickled her nose. "I missed you today, April." He backed up a few inches and looked around, obviously impressed. "Doesn't look like you've had time to miss me, though. Here's a little something for your new apartment." He brought his hidden arm around and presented April with a beautiful bouquet of tiny pink roses, baby's breath and fern leaves.

"Oh, Bob!" April gushed. "They're so beautiful! Thank you!" She held the bouquet out to one side as she crushed Bob with another warm embrace and gave him a half a dozen quick kisses. "I'd better find something to put these in." She started to walk to the kitchen but turned around and took his chin in her free hand, stood on her tiptoes and kissed him again.

He laughed as he removed his jacket, watching her obvious pleasure at his gift. Her appreciation of small acts of kindness made him want to do so much more. His ego swelled at seeing her so delighted at his arrival. He felt like a million bucks.

"Coffee? Or maybe something stronger? I have root beer, too." She laughed from the kitchen. He could hear the joy in her voice.

"I think I need to take the grand tour first." Bob looked around the living room, nodding appreciatively at her furnishings. "I thought we'd be out shopping all weekend, but it looks like you've done it already."

"Not all of it... I had the big stuff picked out this morning and delivered this afternoon. I lucked out with the furniture store. They delivered and set everything up. Check out the bedroom. I can't decide which set of sheets to put on. I need a second opinion." April walked behind Bob, feeling like a schoolgirl again, wanting him to appreciate her homemaking skills, but not wanting to overwhelm him--at least not yet.

Bob flicked the light switch on the bedroom wall. "Nice job, sweetheart! But let me guess...no lights until we get the curtains hung?" April nodded. She walked past him to the closet and tossed the two sheet sets onto the unmade bed.

"I can't decide which pattern I like best. I have the curtains in the bathroom. Wait a sec." She disappeared and returned, holding the curtains for the bedroom. "Okay, which goes better?" She held up the curtain behind the linens on the bed.

"I like 'em both. I'd say you have great taste, honey." He took the few steps to her side, tossed the curtains on the bed and lowered his lips onto hers. "Yep, I was right. Great taste." He nuzzled her neck for a moment before April remembered that they could be seen from the street, and she suddenly broke away. She took his hand and led him out of the bedroom, turning off the light.

"I still have lots of shopping left to do. I was hoping to recruit you into taking me to the department store. Maybe tonight?" His strong arms pulled her close, his hands clasped behind her waist as April leaned her head back, looking into his smoldering dark brown eyes, her arms wrapped around him, very much aware of the electricity that flowed between them. *Is this the power of love?* She wondered. No one had ever given her flowers before. The gift of roses seemed to promise a deeper intimacy to come, a serious invitation from his heart to hers.

"I imagine you could talk me into just about anything," Bob said as he lowered his head closer to hers. April's arms reached around his neck as she stood on tiptoe to receive his kiss. His lips barely brushed hers as they were brought back to reality by a loud banging on the kitchen door.

"Hey, lovebirds! Yoo-hoo!!" Patti called as she rattled the doorknob. "Break it up already! You have company!"

Bob reluctantly released April as she went to the door and opened it to Patti and Max. The women hugged as the men shook hands, and Max handed a brown paper bag to April.

"I believe it's your favorite," smiled Max as April hugged him again.

"Ooh, what's this?" April pulled a bottle of champagne from the paper bag. "It is my favorite. You guys are the greatest...can we open it now?"

"That's what it's for, girlfriend!" smiled Patti. She went to the counter and pulled four Styrofoam cups from a plastic bag. "Let's use the good crystal!"

April handed the bottle to Max. "If you'll do the honors, we'll toast my new apartment and give you the grand tour."

At the popping of the cork, Max poured out the bubbly, and the four friends enjoyed a happy toast to health, long life and prosperity, as Bob and April led the older couple through each room. Patti and Max exchanged knowing glances as April showed off her roses from Bob.

"Now I need this wonderful cousin of yours to take me shopping so I can get a vase for my beautiful flowers." April hinted again, eager to finish decorating and furnishing her apartment.

"Not quite yet, kiddo." They had walked back to the kitchen and Max spoke after a nudge from Patti. "Let's sit down and go over what happened at the store today." His manner suddenly turned serious, and Max took a chair at the table and motioned for the others to do the same.

Bob looked questioningly at April. "What happened today?" he asked slowly, the smile turning his lips into a hard line. He reached for her hand as he spoke. "You should have called me."

"Well, there's even more to tell than what Patti knows," April sighed as she looked at each face around the table, beginning and ending with Bob. "Patti went to pick up our lunch from the sub shop while I stayed at the store. The phone rang and I could hear a television in the background, but I finally hung up because no one spoke. A few minutes later Patti came in with our lunch. While we were eating, the phone rang again and Patti picked it up and gave it to me. At first he didn't say anything, but I could hear a television in the background. As I was going to hang up I heard my name. It was Kenny, calling me horrible names and accusing me of laughing at him." April looked down at her hands. "He said he was going to kill you and Patti and Max—and then me. He started that horrible screaming again, so Patti hung up the phone. As far as I know, he hasn't called back." She looked up at her friend. "He hasn't, has he?" Patti shook her head.

April took a deep breath as she emptied the champagne bottle, topping off their cups. "What I haven't had a chance to tell anyone yet is that I took the car to go grocery shopping after I walked back home from the bookstore. When the clerk walked me out to the car with my groceries I unlocked the trunk and the trunk lid popped up like it always does. Well, I was talking to the boy and not looking where I set down my grocery bag— and—and I found a little surprise..." Telling the story had the same effect on her as living it had the first time. She was glad to be sitting down, because her knees were weak and her hands trembled as she remembered the vicious crunch of the steel jaws snapping into the frozen meat.

Bob leaned across the table. "What surprise, honey?" He gently coaxed.

"There was a trap on the floor of the trunk." She shuddered. "It sprang when I put my grocery bag on it." April felt unwanted tears trickling down her face. She wiped the tears with the back of her hand.

"Oh, my gosh! I had no idea..." Patti got up from the table and got a paper towel for April. "Here, honey." She stood over April, rubbing the trembling girl's back for a moment. "Well? What are we going to do?" she demanded from Bob and Max. "Should we call the Oakwood Police? They need to put him in a mental institution or something. *He's crazy!*" She fumed as she took her seat again.

"Do we need to go lay down the law for that maniac?" Max growled, pounding his fist on the table, his gray brows knit together in anger. "We could teach him a lesson he won't forget any time soon."

April watched Bob's face. He sat back, one arm crossed over his chest, the other pulling on his moustache. "We've got a serious problem with this guy." He pulled a few more times on his moustache before leaning forward, elbows on the table, fingers steepled, choosing his words carefully. He looked directly at Max and asked, "Didn't we clear out everything in April's trunk when we unloaded her car yesterday?" He scooted April from her chair and onto his lap, wrapping his arms around her.

Max's "Oh, no..." filled the silent room as the realization dawned on the four friends simultaneously. Their widened eyes darted worried looks at each other across the table.

Kenny Colt was in town—and he wanted revenge.

Chapter Twenty-Four

Like the invasion of a small army, they descended on the police station that faced the town square. Patti led the way to the deputy on duty, recounting April's ordeal, using her hands as she spoke, with Bob and Max occasionally adding their two cents' worth. April wanted to crawl under the desk and die of embarrassment as the sordid details of her week with a psychopath were retold. Mostly, she feared that Bob would think less of her for going to meet and marry a man she had only known through the Internet, but Bob's strong arm never left her shoulders and he kissed the top of her head every now and then for encouragement as they stood behind the chair that Patti had claimed.

The deputy wrote up his report and assured the foursome that April's apartment would be kept under surveillance. Foot and car patrols would be stepped up until they located her stalker. Located only a few blocks from the police station, she would be in the vicinity of most of the policemen coming and going, and the foot patrolman would check both entryways to her apartment on his beat as well.

As they left the station, Bob told Patti and Max that he would be staying with April until the police located and locked Kenny away, or until they were certain he was back in Oakwood. April breathed a sigh of relief, knowing that steps had been taken for her safety and that Bob would do everything in his power to keep her safe. Patti was reluctant to leave, but Max chided his concerned wife. "Come on, honey. Let's give them a little space. April needs to get those curtains up tonight."

"I don't feel totally safe until they catch that creep, Max." Patti retorted. "What about that saying, 'There's safety in numbers'? April, why don't you and Bob stay with us until they find him?" Max nodded in agreement.

"We'll be okay. Now stop your worrying, Pat!" Bob put his arm around Patti and gently shook her shoulders. "I'll take April to get the curtains and hardware we need. If we don't finish up in every room tonight we'll sleep in the room that's done first. It'll be okay. The police will be watching the place, especially tonight. I don't think we need to worry for the time being."

"Well...okay." Patti reluctantly agreed, "But only if you guys come over for brunch tomorrow. You can get all the curtains up tonight then come straight over to us in the morning, okay?" Patti crossed her arms over her chest, standing her ground, while Max laughed, rolling his eyes.

"You'd better say 'okay,' April. You know how stubborn she gets," Max said affectionately.

April looked at Bob, who nodded in agreement. After Patti was satisfied with the arrangement, the two couples got into their separate vehicles, Patti and Max heading home while Bob and April headed for the department store in his Dodge. When the truck slowed to a stop at the end of the block, Bob looked over at April. "Honey, you'd better scoot over here quick." April did as he said, fearing that Kenny was standing on the corner. She slowly looked at the stop sign, but didn't see anyone. "I think your door's broken." he said.

"It looks okay to me," she said, pulling on the handle to make sure it was locked.

Bob's laughter filled the cab as April realized he was teasing her. "Oh, you! I thought Kenny was out there or something!"

"Nope. Just wanted you sitting next to me." His smile took away the strain she was under. This night would remain etched in her memory forever. Her first bouquet of flowers, being surrounded by her loved ones, and the first time a man used a "line" on her. Despite the menace of Kenny Colt hanging like a blanket over them, April smiled and snuggled closer to Bob as they drove the few miles to the far end of town where the big department stores stayed open round the clock.

Bob pulled into the busy parking lot, which was still bustling with shoppers despite the lateness of the hour. "Here we are." Bob turned and gave April a reassuring kiss before sliding out of his seat and reaching for her as she stepped down to the pavement. They walked hand in hand through the automatic doors, and April realized that Bob had shortened his stride so she could keep up with his long legs. She was growing accustomed to feeling "warm and fuzzy" whenever he was near, feeling full of love for this gentle giant of a man who continually endeared himself to her.

Together, they wandered every aisle in the large store, quickly filling the basket with all the little gadgets that make a house a home. Bob seemed to know what hardware they needed for the curtains, drapes and mini-blinds, so April went to Housewares to replace items that had been left behind in Kenny's shed. She bought enough place settings to serve six, followed by a package of silverware. By the time she had chosen her water glasses, Bob had turned into her aisle, curtain rods sticking out of the cart like a knight's lance. She emptied the items she carried in her arms into the cart and found a set of plain wineglasses to add to her growing mound of items. She found a lightweight steam iron, then an ironing board. Bob pushed the cart, one arm lying across the precariously perched board, as April made her way to the Ladies' Department. She chose a pair of jeans and a pair of khakis, two turtlenecks in black and maroon, navy sweats, and two sweaters to wear with the turtlenecks.

"Are you holding up okay?" she teased Bob. "I think once we've got all this set up, all I'll need is some plants." Bob smiled at her seriousness as she looked through the items in the cart. "Can you think of anything important I've missed?"

"I think you've got most of the store in here." He laughed. "I'll be glad to come back tomorrow and the day after, if we need to." Bob glanced both ways up and down the aisle and saw that they were alone for a moment. "Can you hold this down a minute, honey?" He gestured to the ironing board. April leaned onto the board and Bob took her face in his hands, planting a solid kiss on her startled face. She smiled at the sparkle in his eyes, at his playfulness, and in her eagerness to give as good as she got. The metal ironing board hit the tile floor with a loud bang. April and Bob looked up to see half a dozen faces staring at them. For the second time that night, April's cheeks matched the color of her new turtleneck.

April worried the entire time it took to unload the truck and bring in all the bags. Bob had instructed her to keep watch from the stoop while he made all the trips up and down the stairs. Her fear of seeing Kenny pop out of a dark corner and attack Bob was almost unbearable. She watched carefully as he rummaged through the back of the truck, then locked the Dodge and set its alarm before bringing the last load up. She slowly let out the breath she had been holding when she finally pushed the door closed and securely locked it behind him.

After a quick kiss, they each set to work. As Bob installed the curtain rods in the bedroom, April set up her ironing board and filled the steam iron with water. The black rectangle of the curtainless windows in the kitchen made April feel as though Kenny's hateful eyes were watching her every move. She ironed as quickly as possible and brought the unwrinkled curtains to lie on the bed as Bob finished the last of the bedroom hardware.

"Relax, honey. It's okay." He went to April and held her, his chin resting on top of her head. "See how fast that went? We'll be done in no time."

136

"I feel safe, now that I'm with you. In the kitchen, it feels like he's staring at me from every window." April shuddered. "I'll be all right once these are up."

They made quick work of putting up the lined curtains in the bedroom and decided to do the kitchen next. April had chosen mini-blinds for each window and the door, with a valance and café-style rod for the window over the sink. She ironed furiously as Bob installed the mini-blinds, and soon the kitchen was a private haven, rather than a window to the world. April became progressively calmer and happier as she ran the warm iron over the drapes. She let the iron cool before smoothing out the sheers, and when all the rods had been installed they worked together, sliding the sheers on the smaller rods, then hung up the heavier drapes. Bob worked the cords on the heavy rods and April could see the self-satisfaction in his grin as he repeatedly opened and closed the drapes smoothly.

"What's next, honey?" Bob plopped down on the comfortable couch. "Is there a television or stereo that needs hooking up?"

"I didn't have a stereo and I have no idea what Kenny did with my television. It's almost too quiet in here, isn't it?" April sat down next to Bob. They both put their feet up on the coffee table and Bob's arms automatically wrapped themselves around April. "It feels so good and safe when you hold me."

"You feel good to hold." Even Bob's whispers were like little caresses that April soaked in with her whole being. "This being in love sure feels good, doesn't it?"

April snuggled deeper into his embrace, her heart leaping at his use of the "L" word. She had been afraid to say what she felt in her heart—afraid of scaring him away. "I knew I loved you when you gave me your wool socks and rubbed my feet." She held her breath, waiting for his reaction.

"Is that when you knew? I'll bet you didn't know I've had a thing for you for a couple of months already..." he teased.

"You couldn't have; we just met." April turned to look into his eyes and moved around so she was lying with her head in his lap as he bent over her, cradling her head in one arm and stroking her hair with his free hand.

"Ahh...but you've forgotten the power of Patti..." His words trailed off as he bent to kiss her.

"Patti?" Another kiss. This one tickled her upper lip from his moustache and she giggled. She struggled to sit up straight and sat with her legs crossed "Indian-style" as she faced him.

"Come on, now, 'fess up!"

"Patti's been trying to fix us up for about a year, I'd guess. She waited until I'd been divorced for a while before she even told me about you. Didn't want me dating you on the rebound. She sent me a picture of the two of you from some bookseller's convention." He leaned toward her for a peck on the lips. "I thought you looked like an angel in that picture." He looked deeply into her eyes. "I still have it, too. Carry it around in my wallet." He shifted his weight, pulling his billfold out of his back pocket. "See?" April took the wallet and slowly smiled as she peered at the year-old photo: April and Patti, sporting big smiles, arms around each other at the Boucheron conference. She handed his wallet back to him and leaned forward for another peck.

"That was a happy time. Patti's mentioned you several times, but never hinted about us getting together... Well, maybe that was because I kept telling her that I was happy being single and didn't want a man in my life...until I messed up with that--that..." April felt her face heating up as she recalled her excitement about Kenny. "Bob, I can't believe…"

"Shhhh...It's over, or it will be soon." They leaned towards each other, a deep and passionate kiss erasing all thoughts of Kenny from their minds. When they pulled apart, Bob took April's hands in both of his and looked directly into her eyes, "I love you, April." He gently squeezed her fingers as he said the simple words, his eyes never wavering from hers.

Tears of happiness blurred her vision of the dark pools of Bob's eyes as April whispered, "I love you, too, Bob." They sat for a moment, holding each other, and they started laughing. "Whew! We've both said the 'L' word; now we can get down to business!" They laughed again.

"How about some root beer to toast the beginning of a wonderful relationship?" April offered.

"Sounds great. Too bad we don't have any music for this romantic evening." Bob looked at April with puppy dog eyes. "We could have danced the night away."

"Oh, slow dancing. I'd really like that." April found the package that held the wine glasses and brought them to the kitchen sink to wash. If they were going to toast their relationship with root beer, they should use the good china. "I have some romantic CD's. They were in with the computer things."

"How about if I hook up the computer and we'll get a little mood music going?" Bob stretched to his full height and walked to the kitchen. "I could set it up on the entertainment center." He stood close behind her, encircling her with his arms. "I like having my own real life angel," he whispered in her ear. She giggled as she turned and wrapped her arms around his neck. "And I like having my very own knight in shining armor."

Bob reluctantly released his arms from his sweetheart and went to get the boxes that held her computer and its components. He brought them into the living room and turned on the lights, carefully removing the contents. There didn't seem to be any booby traps or damage done, so he set the tower on a shelf and plugged it in. He attached the monitor, speakers and mouse. A few moments later, he turned it on.

"Ok, honey. We're in business. What do you want to hear first?" Bob stood with several of the CD's in his hands. "How about *Kenny Rogers' Love Songs?*"

"That'd be great." April smiled as she set the wineglasses of root beer on the coffee table. She went to the keyboard and typed in her password, hearing the familiar sound her computer made when the password kicked in. Bob removed the silver CD from its plastic case and slid it into the slot on the tower while April lit the vanilla-scented candle and turned out the living room lights.

As the romantic melody of "You Decorated My Life" filled the room, April picked up the wine glasses and handed one to Bob. They looked deep into each other's eyes in the flickering candlelight and held up their glasses. Bob thought for a moment, pulling on his moustache a few times, and murmured, "To a lifetime of love." They gently clinked glasses, entwining their arms, and took a sip. April was sure the root beer was making her every bit as giddy as a glass of champagne. She felt enveloped in Bob's sweet love as he took her glass and put it on the coffee table. He held her waist in one strong hand and pulled her close. April started off properly positioned for a slow dance, but soon Bob bent a little lower so she could lay her head on his shoulder as they moved together, gently swaying around the living room. They whispered of love and longing and kept moving, even as the song came to an end and another one began. April closed her eyes and felt like a princess. All of her dreams had come true. Her fantasy man had come to life, saved her life, and even wanted a life--with her. Their lips sought each other's in a long, slow, deep kiss that seemed to last a lifetime of its own. Another song came to an end and Bob broke their embrace to pick up their wine glasses. He handed one to April and they clinked a toast, finishing their root beer.

"Some more bubbly, honey?" April asked Bob as she took both glasses and turned to go out to the kitchen. As she turned, April stifled a scream and dropped the wine glasses on the carpet.

She looked straight into the hollow eyes of Kenny Colt.

Chapter Twenty-Five

April gasped in shock, her knees wobbling. She felt the heat of embarrassment rush to her face. "I-I'd forgotten Kenny's picture was my screensaver." April's hand went to her heart as she explained her reaction to a startled Bob. She bent to pick up the wine glasses, but the mood they had shared was now broken as Kenny intruded into their lives once more.

"It's okay, honey." Bob joined her at the kitchen sink as her trembling subsided and she washed out the wine glasses. He picked up the dish towel and dried. They cleaned up in companionable silence, each lost in their own thoughts. Finally, Bob shut down the computer. "We'll take care of setting this up tomorrow. We'll have all day to finish getting you settled in then, okay?" He went to April and held her for a moment.

"I-I feel like such an idiot." April mumbled into his chest. Holding her close to him, Bob smoothed April's hair and rubbed her back, while he silently cursed Kenny Colt under his breath and decided that he needed another visit to the local law enforcement to see that the patrols by April's apartment had been started.

"Why don't you get ready for bed, honey?" Bob looked deeply into April's eyes and held her by the shoulders. "How about if I run a nice hot bath for you? You can relax while I take care of a couple of business calls I've got to make. I'll be back before you know it."

"I think a long, hot soak is just the ticket," April agreed, "but you go on and do what you have to do. I can handle filling the tub." With a quick kiss goodbye, Bob let himself out the back door and stood listening on the back stairs until he heard the reassuring clunk of the deadbolt securing the door.

April started the water for the tub. She poured in an extra capful of her gardenia-scented bubble bath and watched the thick, frothy bubbles multiply under the force of the spray. She hurried to the bedroom for a nightgown, and quickly shed her clothes. She tested the water temperature with her big toe and let the rest of her body slip gently into the warm water. She turned the hot water higher and luxuriated in the heat and smell of her favorite flower, encased in the white foam up to her chin. She sighed deeply and finally relaxed for the first time since her adventure had begun. She went over the details of the past week in her mind. The nightmare that had been the result of wanting something so badly, she had let herself believe a horrible crazy man could be "the one". Her mind quickly switched gears as she remembered her first encounter with "big, bad Bob." How gentle and caring he was. Big, bad Bob—her knight in shining armor. The corners of her mouth turned up into a smile as she turned off the hot water and lay back to soak, relishing her memories of the short time she had shared with this wonderful man. She felt his presence in her heart, along with the certainly that he was sincere. Unlike her feelings for Kenny that she'd had to force herself into believing, the feelings for Bob flowed straight from her heart, as well as her mind. She felt his love and protectiveness like a cloak all around her.

April woke with a start. The bathwater was lukewarm, but it was the sound that cut through the haze of her dreams that had awakened her. She heard the muffled "meows" of a cat. April stood in the tub and grabbed a towel, wiping herself quickly. She crept into the hallway and listened again. This time she heard the poor creature scratching at the front door in the living room. Someone must have let the cat into the front entrance, and now it was trapped in the stairwell. She loved animals and would be glad for the company. She pulled on her socks and underwear, then her new sweat suit. She went first to the back door and looked out into the rear alley. Bob's parking space was still empty, but her Escort gleamed in the reflected streetlight. The cat's persistent meowing drew her to the front door. She peeked through the living room curtains to see if anything looked suspicious on the street below, but all was quiet. There were a couple of cars parked along the sidewalks, but nothing unusual. She held the doorknob in one hand as she turned the deadbolt with the other. The cat mewed and scratched again as April slowly opened the door. Before she could turn on the stairway light, something huge pounced, covering her face and body with a rough blanket. April fought and squirmed, her mind reeling in confusion.

"Hello, darlin'!" She had fallen on her back as someone pushed and rolled her into a thick—what? Blanket? Rug? April's heart skipped a beat as she heard the whiny sarcasm in Kenny Colt's voice.

"Let me out of here!" she demanded as she struggled against the scratchy fabric, but she couldn't find an opening. Her arms were pinned to her sides and she could barely move. Only her feet were free, but she couldn't move her legs apart enough to kick.

"Oh, you'll be getting out all right, sweetheart," Kenny said in his maniacal sing-song voice, "as soon as you've learned your lesson."

"Kenny, let me go! I can't breathe!" April pleaded. "Please." She felt a dull thud at her side and realized Kenny had kicked her, but the heavy fabric not only held her prisoner, it protected her as well.

"Shut up!" Another thud, this one by her head. April felt herself being lifted upright and then lowered to an angled position. After a few movements she realized that she was being carried down the front steps, probably over Kenny's shoulder. She tried to wriggle herself free from her prison, but she couldn't get the momentum to cause him to drop her on the stairs. Somehow, she had to stall for time. '*Bob!*' she silently prayed, "*please hurry.*"

"Why are you doing this? Let me out of here, Kenny! Kenny, I can't breathe! Please!"

If she couldn't get him to drop her, maybe she could make enough noise to get someone's attention. She felt the cold air on her feet and knew she was already on the sidewalk. She was set upright again on an angle and heard a vehicle drive by. "Help me!" she screamed. She could hear Kenny's sick laughter and felt herself being lifted up in the air once more.

"I'll help you darlin'," Kenny crooned. "I'll help you to shut up!" She felt her head being shoved down into an unmoving wall of some sort. Luckily, her prison still held and cushioned her head from whatever assault Kenny had planned for her. She felt she was being twisted pretzel-like and realized that she was being shoved into the trunk of a car.

"No! Kenny, please!" She cried. All she could hear was muffled laughter and the creak of a trunk as the lid slammed down on top of her. There was silence for what seemed like an eternity as April fought hard with her emotions. If she started to cry she would probably suffocate. She had to keep her head clear and deal with this. She was startled by two fast raps on the trunk's hood. Another slam as the driver's door closed. Next, she felt the vibrations as the motor came to life. She rocked gently as the car moved, slowly at first, and then gaining speed as it drove due north into the night.

146

Chapter Twenty-Six

Bob could not shake the feeling that he needed to get back to April. *Now!* The tightness in the pit of his stomach was never wrong, and it was getting stronger. As he waited for Detective Taylor to finish the phone call that had been put through while the two men were discussing April's surveillance, Bob worried that the local police force hadn't taken his earlier visit seriously. The plan was to start the extra drive-bys in the morning, but his gut feeling was telling Bob it should have started much sooner.

Detective Taylor dropped the handset and swiveled in his chair to look directly at Bob, his demeanor grim. "You hit the nail on the head. That call was from the Oakwood Police." The detective let out a loud sigh as he stood and put one beefy hand on Bob's shoulder. "Do you know a Pastor Wilson? Wife's name is Marian?"

"Those are the people that April stayed with before her attack by Colt. Why? Has something happened to them?" Bob rose slowly, more than ready to get back to April's side.

"Colt put 'em both in the hospital. The old man might not make it. His wife was alert enough to give a statement to the police. She was so worried about April, she forced herself to stay conscious." Charlie Taylor finished writing on a memo pad, tore off the top sheet and handed it to Bob. "Here's the make and model of the car he stole. Apparently he's on his way to find her. I'll put out an APB. If he's in town, we'll get him."

The two men shook hands. "Thanks, Charlie. I owe you one." Bob hurried out of the building, practically running to his truck. The feeling in his stomach was stronger. He spun his tires as he raced the few blocks to the apartment. His adrenaline and protective instincts shifted into high gear. He finally found the woman that felt like his "other half," and nobody, but nobody, was going to take her away from him. His truck skidded into its parking space on the other side of the steps to April's back door. The Escort looked fine. The dim light from the kitchen window through closed curtains made a rosy glow, and the back stairway light was on. Everything looked fine.

He took his gun from the back waistband of his jeans, flicked off the safety and pushed the truck door slowly closed so it didn't slam. When his eyes adjusted to the dimness of the night, he surveyed the area and felt safe as he crept to the foot of the wooden stairs and slowly started his ascent. He reached the top step and peeked through the back door's small window. He couldn't see anything out of the ordinary. He tried the doorknob and was relieved to find it still locked. He pulled a duplicate key set out of his shirt pocket and inserted it into the deadbolt. The lock turned and made a muted *clack* as it opened. Inserting the key into the doorknob, the door swung inward, making a high-pitched squeal. Bob's ears perked up, alert to any unusual sounds from the apartment, but there weren't any.

"April?" he whispered.

He quietly shut the door behind him, and as he crept closer to the living room he could see signs of a struggle. The coffee table was up-ended, its candle lying sideways on the kitchen floor. The overstuffed chair was at an awkward angle. He crept to the closed bathroom door, listening for a moment. Nothing. A few more steps and he stood in the bedroom doorway. He flicked on the overhead light and saw no sign of her, the adrenaline pumping harder through his veins. He made a quick search of the closet and looked under the bed. Nothing. He shut off the light and went back to the closed bathroom door. Leaning against the door jamb with the barrel of the gun tilted upward, he turned the knob and pushed with his shoulder. Along with his own look of frustration reflected in the bathroom mirror were large red block letters, a hastily scrawled message in lipstick: "YOU LOSE." Bob closed his eyes and took a deep breath, praying he wasn't too late.

He surveyed the living room to determine how Kenny had gotten April to open the door, but he didn't have a clue. April would never let Kenny near her again, at least not willingly. She had put up a struggle, but thankfully, there was no blood. His instincts told him she was still alive. He locked the front door, went back through the kitchen and down the back stairs. Jumping in the Dodge, he fired it up and flew to the police station.

"Charlie!" He trotted to Detective Taylor's desk. "He's got her. These are the keys to her apartment. See what your guys can find. I'm heading back to his cabin in Oakwood. Radio ahead for me, will ya?"

"You got it. Be careful." Charlie sat back down after catching the keys in mid-air and dropping them on his desk pad. He picked up his phone and flipped through his Rolodex with the other. "Yeah, Oakwood. This is Detective Taylor...we've got an APB..." He gave Bob a "thumb's up."

Bob didn't stick around long enough to hear the rest of the call. He had to get to April before Kenny did any serious harm. *If that psycho hurt one hair on her head…* No! He wouldn't allow his thoughts to run wild and let emotion override his training. He needed to think smarter than Kenny Colt if he was to save his future wife. Future wife! The power of that single thought kicked his need for finding April into overdrive. He would find her. His heart would lead him to her. The adrenaline coursing through his veins made him feel invincible as he planned his attack on Colt. His mind cleared and he knew instinctively where his prey was headed.

Chapter Twenty-Seven

Rolled tightly into the braided rug, April was finding it more and more difficult to breathe. Her humid breath mingled with the fumes from the exhaust of the old car and she had to fight to stay conscious. Her back and legs were aching from the twisted position she was forced to keep, and her left arm had long ago gone numb. Her last thoughts were of Bob and the love she felt for the man who had made her life worth living.

"Dear God," she prayed, "please…" April ceased to care, as the fumes overtook her and the darkness quelled her thoughts.

Bob was deeply lost in his own thoughts when the red lights and blaring siren startled him into swerving onto the shoulder of the highway. The police car aligned itself to Bob's truck as he slowed down and turned the Dodge onto the grassy shoulder.

The state trooper lowered the passenger window of his cruiser and yelled, "You the fella going after April Stover?"

Bob nodded.

"Follow me. I'll be escorting you to Oakwood."

"Yes, sir!" Some of the weight lifted from Bob's shoulders. There was no longer any need to worry about speeding with the resultant waste of precious time as he explained the situation. Red lights flashing, cutting through the black night like a beacon, the cruiser flew down the highway. Bob smoothly guided the pickup back onto the road and watched as his speedometer made a steady climb to 80, then 90 mph. The lights gave him a focal point as his mind wandered back to April and what Colt might be doing to her. The maniac was playing some sort of pathetic "cat and mouse" game, if Bob had interpreted the message on the bathroom mirror correctly—a dangerous game that Colt had already decided he'd won. The thought of April being hurt and helpless ripped through Bob's heart and he had to fight with himself not to imagine the worst as the miles slipped behind him.

Chapter Twenty-Eight

Kenny laughed and talked to himself nonstop from the moment the old car left April's apartment. It had been over an hour that he'd been on the highway to Oakwood, making sure he stayed within the speed limit, not wanting to call attention to himself. Not yet, anyway. The thought suddenly crossed his mind that kidnapping April wasn't as much fun now as it had been when she was fighting with him. He expected her to struggle and hammer on the trunk of the car. She wasn't playing fair at all. Here he was risking everything to have her for himself and the stupid bitch couldn't even give him the satisfaction of getting angry! In the distance, he could make out the green and white of a familiar gas station sign and decided to pull over for a short break. He needed to relieve himself and could use a cold drink too.

He pulled up to the gas pumps farthest from the building, in case she decided to start making a racket while he was in the men's room. He chuckled as he looked around. There wouldn't be too many people out at this time of night. No one pulled in as he unscrewed the gas cap. He leaned against the trunk as he filled the tank. There was no noise coming from the trunk. He finished filling the tank and walked inside to the cashier, who was more interested in the magazine she was reading than in taking his money. After using the men's room he slowly walked through the snack aisles, leisurely choosing a few packs of crackers and donuts, and lastly pulled a soda from the cooler. He walked up to the pimply-faced teenager and handed her some money. He tried to make her look at him with the force of his stare, but the kid wasn't interested in anything but her magazine. He chuckled again as he swaggered out to the car, got in, turned on the lights, and returned to the monotony of the road. He hadn't gone too far when it crossed his mind that something might be wrong in the trunk. There hadn't been a single sound from April since he had stuffed her in there. Or did she still think she was too good for him? Was that it? *He wasn't good enough to talk to?* He began to feel the heat rising from his neck to his face. He wasn't taking any more sass from her. Who did she think she was anyway? Taking off with some guy when she was supposed to marry him! He became so enraged that he slammed his fists on the steering wheel. No more "nice" guy! She could sit up here with him and beg his forgiveness. That lying, sneaking... He slammed on the brakes as he pulled the car off to the side of the road. He pulled the release lever to unlock the trunk and left the keys in the ignition as he hurried around to the back of the car.

He grabbed at the braided rug and jerked one end of it as hard as he could, lifting it free from the trunk. He dropped the end on the ground and heard a muffled moan as he pulled the other side out and let it drop onto the pavement. He kicked at her with his boot, but no other sound came from the rug.

"*Stupid bitch*! *Get up!*" He grabbed the loose end of the rug and unrolled April out onto the pavement. She didn't move. Kenny kicked at her gingerly with the toe of his boot this time, worried that she was dead.

"Baby?" He knelt on the pavement beside her and shook her shoulder. "April? What's wrong, baby?" He smoothed the hair from her face. Her complexion was an eerie white in the moonlight, but he saw her chest rise and fall, so he knew she was still breathing. She began to cough, alternately taking in gasps of air.

"Come on, baby. You're okay." Kenny helped her to her feet and stood her up to lean against the car. "Can you stand right here, baby?" He kept an eye on her as he rolled up the rug and stuffed it back into the trunk. Closing the lid, he said, "You gonna be all right, baby?" April nodded, but didn't move.

"Take a couple of deep breaths," Kenny instructed. She deeply breathed in the sweet, cold air and started to shiver.

"I--I'm freezing," she said. Kenny helped her to the driver's side and pushed her across the seat. He reached over and fastened the seatbelt around her waist as she leaned against the passenger door and nodded in and out of consciousness.

"It's okay, baby. We're going home." Kenny felt a stab of fierce possessiveness toward her. She should have been his wife by now. How could she up and leave him? He shoved a donut into his mouth, put the car in gear and pulled back onto the road. Maybe that guy kidnapped her and she couldn't get away. Maybe... All this thinking was giving him a headache. The hours crawled by until he finally came to the last turnoff before Oakwood and left the highway. He'd decided to take the longer way home on the back roads, in case Pastor was mad at him for borrowing the car. As the old car came to a stop at the end of the exit ramp, Kenny saw red twirling lights flying down the highway. "Poor sucker. Some jerk's in big trouble tonight!" As he took a left over the highway overpass, the state cruiser sailed underneath, a black Dodge following close behind.

Chapter Twenty-Nine

April felt the cold night air hit her hard as she slid sideways out of the car. She blinked her eyes a few times and felt arms grabbing at her in an effort to break her fall. When she realized the arms belonged to Kenny Colt, she went limp and continued her sideway slide into the snow. Kenny muttered and mumbled to himself as he tried to maneuver April's dead weight. When he left her to go back to the rear of the car, she opened her eyes to get her bearings. Her foggy mind gradually cleared and she knew she was back at the cabin. She said a silent prayer that God would keep her from becoming locked inside the cabin with Kenny. With mounting terror, her heart cried out to Bob's, and she couldn't help the sob that escaped from her lips, unheard by her captor as he tossed the braided rug beside her shivering form. He roughly rolled April onto the carpet, grabbed an end and started dragging it toward the front steps of the cabin. April's dead weight and the slushy snow made for slow progress and a maddening amount of effort on Kenny's part. She could hear him panting with his struggle and hoped he would tire out soon. She had to escape, but with no coat and the rapidly dropping temperatures she wouldn't last long if she tried to run away. Even if she did, he'd track her footsteps.

At the bottom of the steps, Kenny stopped to rest for a moment. She heard the rattle of keys and the sound of the padlock snapping open. She peeked through her lashes to get her bearings and thought she saw a movement through the trees, where the country road and the fence line met. Oh, God, please, please let it be Bob, she prayed silently. She strained to see some movement again, but there was only a shadow. Her heart sank as she felt Kenny pick her up under her arms and grunt as he moved backward, dragging her up the steps. She would not help him in any way, even if it meant freezing to death on the front steps of the cabin. When he pulled her all the way over the threshold of the door, he dropped her and started to kick at her legs to move them farther inside so he could shut the heavy wooden door.

She heard a crack and Kenny's surprised scream. "What the?" April opened her eyes and saw Kenny staring in disbelief at his blood-soaked hand. There was a gash at the side of his head and his ear was bleeding! Their eyes met and Kenny's look of surprise turned to hatred. "You bitch! You did this!" Another shot ripped through the cabin, pinging into the tea kettle on the stove. Kenny kicked fiercely at her legs. "You're gonna pay for this, you whorin' Jezebel!" April managed to rise up on her elbows, but the force of his blow to her cheek with his boot knocked her back down. She rolled away to avoid another blow, but Kenny had raced to the back of the cabin.

Shouting obscenities and screaming at April, he was searching for something in the back of the cabin. She tried to crawl back out onto the porch as bullets whirred over her head. Kenny was clanging pots and pans together and screaming something about "kingdom come" when she smelled the unmistakable odor of propane gas.

She cried out into the darkness, raising up on her knees and waving her arms, "No! Stop!" A final bullet flew over her head and through the cabin, scratching along the surface of the cast iron cook stove, creating sparks. The sparks caught the stream of propane gushing from the burners and ignited a fireball that knocked a raging, maniacal Kenny Colt across the bedroom and through its small window, depositing his lifeless form in the low branches of an old oak tree. It whooshed through the living room, picking up April in its fury to exit the cabin, and bounced her limp body across the front yard and into the treed fence line.

Ambulance and Fire Rescue vehicles arrived at the same time the fireball spent itself. A tongue of fire licked along the back side of the house and ate up the outbuildings as the propane tank blew skyward. Bob raced through the snow to kneel at April's side, shielding her from debris that showered the moonlit yard. She moaned when he moved her arm, but she didn't open her eyes. He shouted for the paramedics as the ambulance backed into the yard and held her as they navigated through the snow and brought the gurney, shooing him away until they'd managed to put on a neck brace and slid her onto a backboard, then lifted her onto the gurney. They slid her and the makeshift bed into the rear of the ambulance as a female paramedic radioed in April's vital signs to the doctor in the emergency room. Bob sat to the side by her head, never releasing her hand as tears welled up in his eyes. Had he been too late? He said a silent prayer as he held onto April's hand and brushed his lips against the delicate skin. He watched, and felt powerless to help her as her small, limp hand turned a deep, angry purple.

The ambulance arrived at the hospital, its sirens blaring. A medical team was waiting as the gurney was rolled inside the emergency room. Doctors and nurses hovered over April and pushed Bob outside. He paced back and forth in the waiting room, remembering every detail of their first meeting, how he'd mistaken her for Kenny Colt. How completely deceived and heart-broken she was when he found her. Their trip home, her delight in the new apartment, the fun they had shopping together. The minute she had put her trust in him, he lost her to Kenny--again. Bob went to the doors of the emergency entrance, stood and watched as a second ambulance pulled in, this time without a siren or flashing lights. He watched as the blanket-covered body of Kenny Colt was wheeled past him to the elevator. Someone pushed the button to the lower level— the level that housed the morgue.

He heard a clamor from the hallway. Bob turned and saw Patti running toward him, Max following closely behind. The cousins hugged and Max clasped his shoulder. Bob filled them in on what had happened in the past few hours, glad for the company. Patti alternated between tears of worry and tears of joy that April had been found. Bob sat back and stroked his mustache, deep in thought, as Patti and Max went to the cafeteria to get some coffee. It would be a long night for them all.

A doctor in green scrubs, with a mask and stethoscope hanging from his neck, walked out of the emergency room to the waiting area at the nurses' station. Bob looked up to see a nurse pointing at him and rose to meet the doctor. The two shook hands.

"She's in a coma with head trauma and several broken ribs. There doesn't appear to be any internal damage. Physically, I think she'll recover. Mentally, however, we'll have to wait and see. Her memory may or may not be affected. I suggest you go home and get some sleep. She won't be waking up for at least several hours." The doctor had clapped Bob on the shoulder for reassurance.

"Can I see her?" Bob asked, the pleading in his voice unmistakable.

"The nurses will let you know when she's assigned a room. She'll be in intensive care for a while. She's there now, so go and see her, and then get some rest, son. There's nothing for you to do right now but wait and pray." The doctor shook hands with Bob once again and went back to the nurses' station.

Patti and Max returned with coffee and sandwiches. Bob relayed the doctor's message and set off in search of April. He returned a few minutes later, tears welling up in his eyes, and he refused Patti's offer of food.

The three stayed until each had had a turn visiting April in Intensive Care. Bob went in for a final visit, praying she'd waken when she heard his voice. He took April's small hand in his, trying not to hold it too tightly, and leaned over to kiss her pale lips. "I'll be back in the morning, sweetheart. The doctor said you'll be out for several hours, but I won't be far away. I love you, April." Bob reluctantly joined Patti and Max in the waiting room. With the directions Patti had gotten from a nurse, they left for a nearby motel.

Chapter Thirty

April awoke, shivering. She had kicked off the flimsy hospital covers, and upon waking thought she was lying in snow in front of the cabin. Realization set in and she remembered that she was in a hospital room, safe from whatever had happened to put her there. She leaned forward in the dark to pull the covers back up over her arms and her mind exploded with pictures that appeared like the pieces of a puzzle. She knew the images were all related, but she couldn't quite put them together. She remembered her intense fear of being overpowered in her stairwell. The next moment she was in a dark, confining space, unable to breathe, thinking she would suffocate if she allowed herself to cry. She remembered the fear of being in a cocoon. And only recently, she had an overwhelming sense of comfort and peace on hearing the words, "I love you, April." Bits and pieces of her life came back, always accompanied by a mental effort that made her head pound. She closed her eyes and willed herself to remember the face of the man she loved.

Bob paced the floor of his motel room. He tried to force himself to sleep, but the harder he tried, the more restless he became. What if April awoke during the night? He wanted to be with her when she opened her eyes, if not to comfort her, then to comfort himself. He had called the hospital twice since checking in at the motel, and there was still no change in her condition.

Sitting in the recliner, he pulled back the drapes and stared out into the night sky. From his vantage point he could see the outline of the county hospital. He had been going over the "what ifs" in his mind. What if she never regained consciousness? What if she did, but she didn't know who he was? He needed to be near her. What if she didn't want him around anymore? After all, if he had taken her with him to the police station, April would have been safe. He should have been there to protect her.

Weighed down with guilt, he decided that the only way to atone for what had happened was to be by her side when she awoke, and to promise her that she'd never be alone again—if she wanted anything more to do with him, that is. He sat in the dark in the moonlit room, pulling on his moustache, lost in thought and time, when finally he couldn't stand still any longer. He quickly showered and put on the same clothes, smoothing out the wrinkles in his shirt as best he could. He grabbed his few things from the nightstand and locked the door, walking to the motel office. He paid his bill, left a message for Patti and Max with the desk clerk, and drove back to the hospital.

He walked in through the emergency room entrance, largely unnoticed among people with serious concerns, huddled in the waiting room in small groups of twos and threes. As he approached the Intensive Care area, a male nurse rushed past him into the nurse's lounge, demanding that a doctor be called immediately. Bob made his way past the deserted nurses' station and two more doors before he saw the name "Stover, April." He hoped it was a good sign and that she had been moved to a room and away from the viewing area of the Critical Care nurses. Physically, at least, she would be okay. He slowly pushed the door open and stepped inside, letting the door close softly behind him. There was a dim overhead light that shone down on her sweet face. With her head leaning to one side on the pillows, her dark hair framed her pale features. Several strands were draped across her forehead, and despite the neck brace and angry purple bruises on her otherwise smooth cheek, he was struck by her quiet beauty. He leaned over to brush the hair from her face and saw that she had been crying. He bent to kiss away her tears, his heart in his throat, and again he whispered, "I love you, April." Bob crossed the room and brought the lone chair to the other side of the bed where there was no monitoring equipment. He removed his jacket and slung it over the back of the chair. He gingerly took her hand and held it in his before kissing her gently on the lips. Still holding her hand, he sat in the chair and lay his head on the bed beside her. Finally, he was able to sleep.

Bob awoke with a start, looking into a sea of unfamiliar faces. A doctor was stooped over April, listening to the stethoscope he was moving around over her chest. The male nurse who had passed him earlier in the hallway stepped in between him and April, rolling an IV drip into position beside the bed. Bob was pushed out of the way as the medical team hovered over April and was shortly joined in the corner of the room by a surprised Patti and Max. Patti had her husband's and Bob's hands gripped in each of her own. "I knew she'd be okay." Patti beamed, happy tears streaming down her cheeks.

The trio couldn't see what was happening, but they all were elated when they heard April answer the doctor's questions. Two men entered the crowded room: a deputy sheriff and an Oakwood Detective. They asked questions as the medical team dispersed. Bob remained in the corner, overwhelmed at the depth of feeling he had for April. Patti rushed to April's side, pulling Max along in her eagerness to hug and fuss over her badly-bruised best friend. April was happy to see them both, but when she saw Bob coming from the shadows, her face lit up the room. She lifted her arms to Bob and he enveloped her with his own, kissing her lips, her eyes, her hair. Patti looked at Max and smiled, then nodded towards the door. As they started to leave the room, they heard April whisper, "Big, bad Bob. You found me."

"I had to find you, sweetheart. Life wouldn't be worth living without you."

"What's this?" Patti leaned back into the room. "Is 'big, bad Bob' talking mushy?"

"You'd better get used to it, cousin, because if I'm not mistaken, I hear wedding bells," Bob announced. He looked deep into the eyes of his future bride, the owner of his heart, and saw the happy tears that glistened in April's eyes.

"Well, if that don't beat all." Max said, knitting his eyebrows together as he took stock of Patti's open stare. "I believe this woman's finally speechless!"

THE END

Printed in the United States
57846LVS00002B/148-216